Praise for THE CASCADE KILLER

"Phillips tells a masterful tale that is engaging, endearing and suspenseful. It is rich with local knowledge of central Washington and the Cascade Mountains, two places the author is intimately familiar with. Once I started, it was hard to put the book down. A page-turner for sure."

--Pat Hoglund, publisher of *Western Hunting Journal*, *Traveling Angler*, and *Salmon & Steelhead Journal*

"Real! Captivating! Once you start, you can't put it down! *The Cascade Killer* is VERY well done!"

--Scott Haugen, host and producer of *The Hunt* and author of numerous outdoor books

"Yakima outdoor writer Rob Phillips knows his woods, waters and wardens, and it shows as he weaves them into this fast-paced, gripping murder mystery. You can practically smell the ponderosas and pack horses among pages that seem to leap straight out of the gazetteer. Mixing good old fashioned game wardening with current events, Phillips highlights the complex, often lonely and very vital work Washington fish and wildlife police perform, and a modern national travesty, the high number of missing or murdered native women."

--Andy Walgamott, editor, *Northwest Sportsman* magazine

"Rob Phillips' intimate knowledge of Washington State's outdoors scene and recent newsworthy events is on full display in this fast-paced novel. Featuring a smart, hard-working fish and wildlife officer, a demented serial killer, an attractive FBI agent and a scene-stealing Labrador retriever, this is a great read and if you are like me you'll have a hard time putting this book down!"

--John Kruse, host and producer of *Northwestern Outdoors Radio*

THE CASCADE KILLER

THE
CASCADE
KILLER

A LUKE MCCAIN NOVEL

ROB PHILLIPS

LATAH
BOOKS

Book design by Gray Dog Press and Kevin Breen
Cover image derived from Adobe Stock photos

ISBN: 978-0-9997075-8-6
Cataloging-in-Publication Data is available upon request

Manufactured in the United States of America

Production by Gray Dog Press
www.graydogpress.com

Published by
Latah Books, Spokane, Washington
www.latahbooks.com

The author may be contacted at yakimahunter@yahoo.com

DEDICATION

To Terri, thank you for being there beside me during this endeavor and everything else we have been through over the past forty-two years.

And to my sons, Kyle and Kevin, thanks for being my sounding board and for all your support and encouragement during the writing of this book. It wouldn't have happened without you guys.

Also, to the great dogs that have shared my outdoor adventures over the past fifty years. Jack is a compilation of you all.

PROLOGUE

"There's a bear," Tanner Jamison hissed from behind his binoculars.

Washington's spring bear hunting season had just opened and Tanner, along with his father, Eric, were watching a clear-cut where they had seen bears on two pre-season scouting trips. They had been looking at the edges of the clear-cut when Tanner spotted an odd black object he thought was a burned stump, until it moved. After a few minutes of watching the bear, the two put together a plan they hoped would get them to within 250 yards of the bruin. And then they were off.

The stalk worked out to perfection. It took them longer than they estimated, as the hillside dropped straight down into a small creek that was overgrown with alders and brush, making the walking almost impossible. But they made it through, and after a climb to their predetermined shooting spot, they crept up to the break of the hill and again started searching the clear-cut with their binoculars.

"There it is," Eric said after about thirty seconds. "He's coming out from behind that little fir tree, just up from where we saw him before."

Tanner went prone, using his backpack as a rest. With one shot from his Ruger 7mm, the bear dropped and didn't move.

"Great shot, son!" Eric said excitedly, patting his son on the back.

The elation would last only until they started field dressing the animal. After Tanner accidentally nicked the bear's stomach with his knife, they stared in disbelief at the contents that came oozing out.

"What the heck?" the elder Jamison said as he stared at the bloody mix of meat and grass coming out of the dead bear's stomach. Floating in the gunk appeared to be a human ear.

His son gagged a few times and said, "That can't be an ear, can it?"

As the stomach's contents kept draining out, there were pieces of blue mixed in with the blood-red bile and goo.

"I think it is," said Eric. "And that blue stuff looks like shards of clothing."

"Do you think the bear killed someone and ate them?" Tanner asked.

"I don't know, but we need to call 911 right away."

CHAPTER 1

Interstate 5 heading south out of Olympia was one big traffic jam just about any time. It was no different this day. In fact, if anything, it might have been worse. Luke McCain looked ahead at the long string of cars, all with their brake lights shining red, and felt like screaming. After spending two days in Olympia he wanted to get out of this rat race and be home in time to see his dog and finally get some good sound sleep in his own bed. Unfortunately, the way the bumper-to-bumper traffic was moving on the six-lane, it might be morning before he made it back to Yakima.

As a veteran police officer with the Washington Department of Fish and Wildlife, McCain had been in Olympia for meetings with other fish and wildlife officers from around the state. The meetings were held quarterly so officers from each of the six regional headquarters could train and discuss any trends in the world of fish and wildlife protection.

He was thinking about the meetings and how he was looking forward to getting back to the east side of the state when he glanced down at the speedometer. Was he really going 22 miles an hour in a 70?

"Come on!" he yelled as he pounded the palm of his hand on the steering wheel.

Traffic finally started picking up faster than funeral procession speed around Grand Mound, and by the time he hit Centralia he, along with about 900 other cars, were doing close to the speed limit. With another two hours or more on the road before he got home, McCain decided to stop in Chehalis to grab a burger and get rid of some of the liquid he'd consumed during the meetings that morning.

At six foot, almost five inches and 227 pounds, in top shape from a regular workout routine that included both cardio and weightlifting, McCain made a pretty daunting first impression. He had worked hard at making himself someone that only the very stupid or very drunk would want to mess with.

People in police work put their lives on the line every day, but what the general public didn't realize was that fish and wild-life police officers, or game wardens as many people still called them, were maybe at the highest risk of them all. Studies showed that nearly eighty percent of the people they contacted every day, including many anglers and virtually all hunters, were armed. That, and the desire to be able to hike some of the mountains he hunted each fall, kept him motivated to stay fit.

McCain pulled into the Wendy's in Chehalis and ordered a double with cheese, hold the onions and pickles, with fries and a Frosty. He was calculating how many more miles he was going to have to run to work off those calories when his phone rang.

The screen read YAKIMA COUNTY SHERIFF.

"McCain," he said into the phone.

"Is this the rifleman?" the scratchy voice asked.

"I wish you'd stop calling me that," McCain said.

At thirty-seven, McCain was too young to have ever watched the 1950s TV series that starred Chuck Connors as a lawman in the old west. Instead of a sidearm, Connors used a special lever-action Winchester to handle all his shooting business. And business was good in the weekly series. There was always a bad guy or two who needed gunning down. Connors' character's name was Lucas McCain, and the TV show was called *The Rifleman*. Somewhere along the line, one of the older deputies in the sheriff's department had noticed the WDFW enforcement officer shared his name with the TV character and the nickname landed, whether the real-life McCain liked it or not.

"Yeah, yeah," the deputy on the other end of the line said. "This is Williams. We got a strange one developing up near Chinook Pass and we're definitely going to need some assistance from you and that spoiled dog of yours."

"Oh yeah? Whatcha got?"

"Some hunters shot a black bear this morning and while field dressing it discovered a human ear in the bear's stomach," Williams said.

"An ear? Where's the rest of the body?" McCain asked.

"That's the unknown. It looks like there were some particles of clothing in the stomach contents too, but there weren't any other identifiable body parts the hunters could see. They did say it was a bloody mess."

"It's rare for a black bear to attack a human, but I guess it could have happened."

"Hard to tell, but you think Jack could backtrack the bear to whatever might be left of the body?"

"Probably. It'd definitely be worth a try. I'm in Chehalis, on my way home from Olympia. Even with light traffic over the pass, I'm still two hours from Yakima. I have to grab Jack, so it'll be closer to three. And we'll be losing daylight pretty fast by then."

"Just get here as quick as you can," the deputy said and clicked off.

McCain grabbed his food, jumped in his rig and headed down I-5 to the cutoff to Yakima via Highway 12. As he drove he thought more about the call from Williams. Hearing of someone finding human body parts in a bear's stomach was a first for him. He wondered how it had happened.

McCain had subconsciously bumped his speed up as he pondered the ear in the bear. When he looked down he was doing twenty over the limit in this stretch of the highway. He was driving his state-issued police truck which included a siren and lights in the grill, but he had decided they weren't necessary. The WDFW insignia on the doors of his tan truck would tell the State Patrol and local deputies he was a brother law enforcement officer, but as he thought more about the details he'd received from Williams he went ahead and turned on the lights and pushed the F-150 a bit harder.

As he approached each little settlement along the way, he'd slow some and then roll along about eighty miles per hour until he hit the next small town. Once he hit Randle, he intentionally slowed and really watched the edges of the highway. From here to Packwood and beyond, a large and growing herd of elk had taken up residence, and they loved feeding in the grass along the highway. The last thing he needed right now was to smack a 600-pound elk. First, he would never live it down in the circles of his fellow WDFW officers, but more importantly, he didn't need to be delayed by a collision with a critter nearly the size of a horse.

He made good time getting over White Pass and soon was pulling into the driveway of his house. McCain lived just outside of Yakima in an area known as Lower Naches. When he parked the truck he looked over at the neighbor's house and out the door came a blur of yellow and gold. His dog Jack stayed with Jessie

Meyers and her son Austin when McCain had to overnight out of town. He was thankful for this option, rather than having to kennel his dog someplace. Twelve-year-old Austin loved Jack and treated him probably better than McCain did. The boy played fetch with him, and Jessie was a sucker for Jack's big brown Labrador retriever eyes. All Jack had to do was gaze at her with a longing look, and she'd give him a bite of cookie or some other treat that he'd gobble up.

"Hey, boy," McCain said as the dog came over and got the obligatory belly rub, ear scratch and a few hugs around his neck.

Jack was a big Lab, tipping the scales at just over 100 pounds. And it wasn't a soft hundred. He was solid as a rock, strong as an ox, and could run down a wounded rooster pheasant in nothing flat. He'd come into McCain's life as an eight-week-old ball of fur, with feet too big and soft floppy ears. As they always do, the pup grew fast, and Jack was soon in training to be not only McCain's hunting dog but his partner in wildlife protection.

"What have you guys been up to?" McCain asked the dog.

"We've been playing fetch," said Austin, who had followed the dog out the door. "And Jack's been napping too. You know . . . the life of a dog."

With a mop of brown hair on top of his head, the sides cut short, and the gangly build of an active boy on the verge of being a teenager, Austin was your typical country kid. If he wasn't shooting baskets at the hoop and backboard in his driveway, he was throwing a baseball or a football with one of his buddies. With all the video games, computers, and phones that kids were into now, McCain liked seeing Austin outside getting some exercise and playing with friends.

Occasionally, McCain would play catch with Austin, and he would take him fishing over to the river near their houses. Austin's father had divorced his mother three years before and wasn't around much, so McCain tried to give the boy some guy time as often as his schedule allowed. Of course, it helped that there was a pretty good attachment that had developed between Austin and Jack.

"I do know how dogs are," McCain said as he handed Austin a fifty-dollar bill. "Thanks so much for looking after Jack. And please tell your mom thanks too. I'd like to hang and chat, but Jack and I are needed up near Chinook Pass right away."

"Really?" Austin asked. "What's going on?"

The neighbor boy was always interested in what McCain was doing with his job.

"Don't know all the details yet, but as soon as I know, I'll fill you in. Thanks again, Austin." He patted his right hand on his thigh, and Jack fell in at heel, right next to McCain as he headed to his house.

Ten minutes later, with the big yellow dog sitting next to him in the passenger seat of the Ford pickup, McCain backed out of the drive and headed west. In the quick turnaround in the house, McCain had changed out of his standard uniform—khakis and a tan button-up shirt with his name stitched on one side, his WDFW badge on the other—and jumped into what he called his "field" uniform. He still wore a tan shirt with badge, but he had put on his Wranglers and his favorite pair of Kennetrek hunting boots. His daily uniform also included his utility belt which he always wore. The belt held his holstered Glock semi-automatic pistol in .45 caliber, an ASP collapsible baton, pepper spray, a Taser, a flashlight, and handcuffs.

As he headed out the door he also grabbed his backpack, ready to go in a moment's notice. The backpack included just about everything a person might need to survive a night or two in the mountains. The pack held raingear, an extra couple layers of polar fleece, a waterproof stocking hat and gloves, some freeze-dried food, three bottles of water, a backpacker's stove, a few energy bars and some special dog bars for Jack. For safety and communication he carried a GPS unit for marking and tracking his movement, a handheld radio, and his cell phone. In the storage bin in his truck, McCain always kept a sleeping bag rated to minus 20 degrees, a packable one-man waterproof tent, a down vest and a heavy coat. If he thought he was going to need that stuff tonight, there was room in the pack for it too.

"What do you think, boy?" McCain asked Jack as they ran west on Highway 410. The dog turned and looked at him, barked once, and then went back to watching the road.

McCain had a pretty good idea where the hunters had shot the bear. This time of year, it was difficult to get high in the Cascades because of the snowpack. Some years there was only a few feet in the higher elevations while in other years, like this one, there was thirty feet or more. It had started snowing in mid-November, and a continual parade of storms swinging around from the Gulf of Alaska had dumped snow in the mountains off and on for three months. The deep snow in the high elevations wasn't a problem for the wildlife. They migrated down to lower elevations where normally the snow was either manageable or non-existent. It was on those years when the deep snow hit in the lower elevations, and, combined with persistent below-freezing temperatures, stayed for a couple months or more that created winter mortality with the deer and elk.

Warmer temperatures in February and March meant the snowline had receded to about the 2,300-foot elevation, and it was McCain's guess that the hunters had found their bear in that zone. It was the time of year the bears were coming out of hibernation, and they would actively be feeding to restart their digestive system after being shut down for a few months. During this time most bears will eat grasses and roots, along with the occasional grub if they can find them. Sometimes they'll even feed on carrion—any dead animals that, for whatever reason, didn't make it through the winter. Most bears still have some fat stored as they come out of hibernation, so they don't have to eat. But even then, most are hungry. Evidently the bear that had been killed by the hunters was one of those hungry ones.

McCain turned off the two-lane highway onto Forest Road 1705, known as the Gold Creek Road. The group of law enforcement folks had gathered at an old elk camp on a flat on the ridge just short of Summit Spring. After fifteen minutes of climbing on bumpy, twisty-turny roads, McCain finally saw smoke rising from a campfire just ahead. There were three county sheriff rigs and a WDFW rig parked in the flat. He knew that fellow WDFW officer Stan Hargraves would be here. Williams had told him that. In fact, Hargraves had recommended that the Yakima County Sheriff's Office call McCain.

The three sheriff deputies at the campfire were Williams, a tall and lean man of about fifty, and Paul Garcia, a shorter and rounder man of about forty-five who McCain also knew. When the two stood close together they looked like a lowercase letter "b" or "d" depending on whether Williams was on the left or right side of Garcia. The third deputy, a man of about six feet, in his thirties and fairly fit, was one McCain hadn't met before.

When Jack saw the gathering, he stood up in the passenger seat and started wagging his tail and whining. As they got closer to the group, McCain could see two other people, a man and a teenager. He assumed they were the hunters who had taken the bear. McCain parked, grabbed his jacket, and let Jack jump out to greet the men at the campfire.

"Hey, Jack," Hargraves said. "You ready to earn your keep?"

Jack just wagged his tail and started sniffling around the ground to see if anyone had accidently dropped a bite of cookie or candy bar.

"Sorry, guys. I got here as soon as I could," McCain said to the group. "How did you get here so quickly, Stan?"

Hargraves, who had been at the same meetings in Olympia, said, "I came straight here from the capital. I didn't have to get a mangy dog."

"This is Jeremy Stratford," Williams said pointing to the third deputy.

"Luke McCain," McCain said to the officer. "You must be fairly new? I thought I knew all the Yakima deputies."

"I've been here for a little over a year," Stratford said. "Been in training and on patrol out on the reservation."

"Good to meet you," McCain said and turned to Williams. "So what's the plan?"

The sheriff's office had taken the original phone call, and as senior officer on site, Williams was in charge of the investigation.

"I know it's getting dark," Williams said. "But I think we need to get back to the bear with Jack as soon as possible."

Stratford had arrived a short time before McCain, but Williams and Garcia had already been to the kill site. And, of course, the Jamisons knew right where the bear was, so the senior Jamison was asked to take the lead. Once everyone was geared up and ready to go, they started down the trail. McCain grabbed his backpack, threw in the extra coat, but decided to leave the tent and sleeping bag.

The group only had to go a mile or so, but with the darkness and terrain it took them almost an hour to make the hike. During the walk in, the Jamisons went step-by-step through the story of how Tanner had been drawn for the bear tag, how they'd done some scouting, where they'd spotted the big bear, and how they'd made the stalk and the shot. After shooting the bear, the Jamisons had skinned it, broke it down into quarters, and put the meat in cheesecloth-style game bags to help keep it clean and cool. After talking to the sheriff's office dispatcher, they left the meat where they'd butchered it.

Both Williams and Garcia confirmed what the Jamisons believed they had discovered. Before they had hiked back to the truck to meet McCain, they had photographed the ear, the other contents of the stomach, and everything else in and around the dead bear.

Unlike grizzly bears that would occasionally attack humans, especially if they were protecting cubs, their smaller and blacker cousin, *Ursus americanus*, rarely attacked people. But it did happen. McCain remembered reading about a situation a few years back where a black bear, for no particular reason, had killed a man up in Alaska. He wasn't sure what had happened up here in the mountains of Central Washington, but he definitely wanted to get a better look before drawing any conclusions.

CHAPTER 2

The ear looked like, well, an ear. A left ear to be exact. A small, slimy ear with a bit of the lobe missing. It was difficult to determine if it was an ear from a Caucasian, a Hispanic, a Native American, or an African American, as it was discolored on the upper half and very washed out on the lower half.

McCain knelt and, without disturbing any of the bear's other organs and assorted innards the Jamisons had stacked into a neat little pile, he looked closely at the ear.

"I'd say it came from a woman," he announced to the group standing in a circle and shining their flashlights and headlamps at the severed ear.

"How's that?" Williams asked.

"I'm pretty sure there is a piercing right at the outside of the middle of the ear," he said. "You know, like the girls who work at the coffee stands all have. And, I'm guessing there had been at least one in the lobe right where it is torn."

Williams got in close, took a look, and said, "I believe McCain has something there."

The other guys, including the Jamisons, took turns, one by one, and looked at the ear closely. To a man, and a teenager, they agreed. Yep, those were piercings.

"Not that a man's ears couldn't be pierced like that," said Garcia. "I've seen some guys with some pretty crazy piercings. Have you seen the picture of the dude on the internet that looked like he tripped and fell face first into a fishing tackle box? There's stuff sticking out everywhere."

"That's true," Tanner Jamison said. "There's this one kid at our school who wears a three-piece suit every day, carries a briefcase and has about seventeen piercings on his face. Nice guy, he's just a little different."

"And that blue cloth looks like denim, from a jacket or jeans," McCain said. "We're definitely looking for a body."

"That's why we wanted you up here," Williams said. "Do you want to try tracking with Jack tonight?"

Other police agencies in Washington State used dogs for certain details, and so did the Department of Fish and Wildlife. They had a couple Karelian bear dogs at their disposal for certain tasks. Mostly those dogs were used to bark and harass animals such as bears and wild cats upon their release back into the wild, after having been rehabilitated in captivity. The unique little dogs have incredible reflexes and can harass the animals without harm to the released animals or themselves. The Department also used dogs at the state borders to sniff out potential issues with vehicles bringing contraband into the state. Mostly the WDFW dogs were used at boat inspection sites where they checked for zebra mussels and other invasive species coming into Washington.

McCain figured he could train Jack to sniff out zebra mussels if that was required, but so far the dog had only been asked to find the occasional four-legged creature. Asking him to trace the wanderings of a now dead black bear was going to be a challenge, but it might be the only way they were going to find the person who was now missing an ear and some clothing. Luckily, the snow in the area had only been gone for a few days, and with the wet soil, McCain figured he might be able to help keep the dog on the trail with his own tracking skills.

"My guess is that the bear ate the ear, and whatever other parts of the person, in the twelve hours before Tanner shot it," McCain said. "So, hopefully he didn't travel too far from where the body might be."

"Do you really think someone was up here hiking or something and got attacked by the bear?" Stratford asked.

"I don't," said Hargraves. "It just never happens."

"I agree," McCain added. "But until we find a body, we won't know for sure."

"I had dispatch run a check on any missing persons in Yakima County over the past seventy-two hours," Williams said. "The only missing person was an elderly man who had dementia. I don't believe this is him."

"Coulda been someone from the other side of the hill," Hargraves said.

They all paused and thought about that for a minute, then decided that Eric and Tanner Jamison would help the officers pack the bear meat, hide, and innards out to the trucks for transportation to Yakima. From there the sheriff's deputies would figure out where to send some of the bear meat and brain material for testing, just in case it had attacked someone.

The human ear and shreds of material, packaged separately, along with the rest of the stomach contents, would most likely be sent to the Washington State Patrol crime lab to start DNA testing to see if, at some point, they might find a match to a person missing from sometime before the past seventy-two hours.

The younger Jamison looked a little disappointed that he wasn't going to be taking any of the meat or the hide from the bear home, but Hargraves assured him that once the testing was done, he should be able to have the hide and meat, and that they would take extra good care of it. With that, the men shouldered their packs full of meat, hide, guts, and human remains, and huffed off back up the hill.

McCain turned to Jack and said, "Okay, let's go to work."

A three-quarter moon was coming up over the trees from the east when McCain put Jack on the few tracks he had found of the bear downhill from where it had succumbed to the well-placed shot by Tanner Jamison. The added moonlight helped McCain with his tracking. It didn't matter to Jack. He used his super-sensitive nose to start backtracking the bear.

Scientists believe that the sense of smell for some dogs, such as bloodhounds and other tracking dogs, is at least 1,000 times stronger than a human's. And some dogs' sense of smell is so strong it can still smell a trail up to 300 hours old. McCain didn't know if Jack's olfactory capabilities were as good as a bloodhound's, but he did know the dog could flat track. And he knew the bear's tracks were less than eight hours old based on when the Jamison boy killed the bruin.

Watching the dog work slowly downhill through the edge of the clear-cut, methodically picking up the scent, McCain was confident that Jack was on the trail. Before they started, McCain had the elder Jamison, who was packing the bear hide out to the trucks, kneel down so Jack could get one more good snoot-full of what the big bruin smelled like.

McCain kept his powerful headlamp pointed on the ground and carefully followed Jack as he worked the scent. Occasionally he would bend down and check even the slightest impressions he saw in the soft dirt to confirm that Jack was on the trail.

It took them about two hours of slow, steady tracking before they found the body. Or what was left of the body. The bear had done a pretty good job of spreading stuff around as it had tried to bury what was left of the body under some leaves, grass, and pine needles.

From what McCain could tell, his analysis of the ear had been correct. The body was that of a woman, based on the long black hair and what looked to be bright orange fingernail polish on one of the fingers. He didn't want to be poking around too much, because right now this was a crime scene. His job had been to find the body, and now that that was done, he needed to get back to his truck and call it in.

Before he headed back, he took a few minutes to study the scene. He thought the wounds in the woman's chest looked too neat to have been caused by the bear, but he would wait to hear what the county coroner came up with before he started sharing his thoughts. One thing he knew for sure: the bear hadn't killed this woman. With what McCain knew about the snow and temperatures this area had received during the past few months, it was a pretty good assumption the body had been here for a while, and the below-freezing temperatures had kept the body fairly well-preserved. The deep snow had protected it from birds and other scavengers.

McCain finally stepped back several feet, sat down, turned off his headlamp and took in the night. Jack came over and stuck his head under McCain's arm, which meant he was looking for some petting. McCain obliged.

"Jack," he said while rubbing the dog's ears. "You done good!"

He reached into his backpack and grabbed an energy bar and a bottle of water and shared both with Jack. They ate and drank and listened to the sounds of nighttime in the spring woods.

As he prepared to make the hike back to the truck, McCain pulled out his phone, took several photos of the body and the surrounding area, and then he took off his coat and his shirt and stripped off his cotton undershirt. He draped the undershirt over the bush closest to the body. Then he took a few steps away and urinated in several spots.

It would be tomorrow morning before the crime scene people could get up here, and the last thing he needed was for some other animals, maybe another bear, or more likely a coyote or two, to come in and make more of a mess of what was left of the body. The undershirt would definitely smell like man, based on the day he had had, and the urine should also help keep the critters away. He had done this several times before when he had to leave elk or deer meat overnight in the woods.

McCain put his shirt and coat on, pulled his pack over his shoulders and started for the truck.

"Hold on, Jack," he said to the dog as he started to move out ahead of him. He'd almost forgotten to make a waypoint of the body site in his GPS. He knew he could find the spot again, but just for safety's sake, he got the waypoint marked. If by some chance he wasn't able to come back and lead the crime scene team in tomorrow, they'd have the waypoints that they could follow.

"Now we can go," he said to the yellow dog, and off they went into the night.

CHAPTER 3

The next morning, as McCain and Jack returned home after guiding the crime team to the body, Austin Meyers was the first one to meet them in his driveway.

"So, now can you tell me what happened?" the youngster asked. "Did Jack help you find a hurt animal?"

"Well, Jack did help, but it wasn't a hurt animal he found," McCain explained. "It was the body of a dead woman, who had been partially eaten by a bear."

"Really?" Austin asked. "And Jack found her? Cool."

"He didn't actually track the woman," said McCain. "He tracked the bear backwards from where it had been shot by a hunter. But it would have taken a lot longer to find her without Jack."

Austin was kneeling down next to the yellow dog, and after hearing what Jack had done, he gave the dog a big hug and said, "Wow, you're a hero, Jack. You deserve a treat." And with that, boy and dog were sprinting to the Meyers' house for a cookie or some other sweet Jack didn't need.

"Oh, I see how you are," McCain said to Jack as he ran away with the boy.

As the days went by, officials were considering the death "questionable" but weren't coming right out and saying it was a homicide. Unlikely as it was, it still could have been an accident. They just didn't know.

McCain continued his normal duties, like checking on anglers fishing in the area ponds and lakes. Late April was one of the busiest times for fishing in the region. The local WDFW fish hatchery crews were stocking trout in all the local lakes, and anglers were going after them with a fever. He wrote a few citations to anglers for fishing without a current license, or for keeping more fish than the daily regulations allowed.

The spring turkey hunting season had opened on April 15. There were a few wild turkeys in the region, so he tried to check on the turkey hunters when he could, just to make sure everyone was legally licensed and had taken only birds with a visible beard. He talked to a few hunters, but only checked two who had actually killed a turkey.

One day McCain was working up in the Wenas Valley, in the Wenatchee National Forest to the northwest of Yakima, checking on any turkey hunters who might be in the area. As he drove up the forest service road, he met a car coming down. The driver wasn't in camo clothing, he was driving a silver 90s-era Honda, and he just didn't look like a hunter, which made McCain wonder for a half-second what the guy was doing up there.

McCain slowed and pulled off the one-lane road to let the car pass. He thought the driver might stop and chat for a moment, but he didn't. He just waved and motored right on by. McCain thought about turning around and running the guy down, but he really had no reason to do that, so he let it go and continued up the pothole-filled dirt road, looking for the rare turkey hunter.

Higher up, McCain found a hunter just getting back to his truck. Dressed in camo clothing from head to toe, the man, who was in good shape for someone who looked to be in his 70s, was obviously a turkey hunter. McCain pulled in and climbed out of the truck.

"How you doing?" he asked the hunter.

"I've been better," the man said. "I just missed the biggest tom of my life! Right over there."

"Sorry to hear that. Do you hunt up in this area often?"

"Not much, no. I usually hunt up by Colville, but I live in Yakima and didn't have time to drive up north to hunt, so decided to try up here today. I came in last night right at sundown and heard a couple of gobblers and figured I was in the chips. And it worked too. I called him right in. Well, after trying to get ahead of him most of the morning, I called him right in."

"Not many turkeys up in this neck of the woods," McCain said. "You're lucky to have found some."

"Yeah, I guess so," the hunter said.

McCain asked to see his license, which the man had ready to show him. His name was John Ferguson.

"Everything looks in order, Mr. Ferguson. Sorry you missed the turkey."

"Yeah, well, that happens. The worst part of it is, now the old boy will be educated. All the calling in the world won't get him to come in again."

"Well, maybe you can find another eager tom. Say, you didn't happen to see a guy in silver Honda up this way, did you?

"You know, I did. Didn't look like a hunter though. He just drove right by me when I was walking alongside the road a ways back. Kinda weird having a small sedan like that up here on these rough roads."

"That's what I thought. He might have been up here mushroom hunting or something."

"I guess," Ferguson said. "He was wearing a black cowboy hat. Maybe he was up here looking for lost cattle?"

"In a Honda? Oh well. You have a good day and hope you find another willing tom."

CHAPTER 4

It took eleven days for the county coroner to identify the woman McCain and Jack had found. He had used dental records to identify her, and DNA samples confirmed it. Her name was Emily Pinkham. She was twenty-seven years old and a member of the Yakama Nation. Her last known residence was in White Swan on the Yakama Reservation.

The coroner couldn't make any clear conclusion as to how she had died, nor could he figure out when she had perished. McCain had been right in his assessment of the situation. The cold and snow had kept her body in pretty good shape, that is until a hungry black bear had stumbled across it.

Over the past decade there had been eighteen mysterious disappearances of Native women in Washington State, and when Emily Pinkham went missing in late October the previous year, local authorities made a concerted effort to find her. But it was to no avail. Nobody had seen her with anyone suspicious. And the last person to see her alive, her cousin Jeanine Washut, said she was on her way to work at Legend's, the Yakama tribal casino in Toppenish. Emily worked as a waitress at the buffet restaurant inside the casino. When she missed work for a couple of days, the missing person alert went out, and authorities went on the search.

The problem with missing and murdered Native women had become such an issue in Washington, and around the country, that the governor of Washington State and the U.S. Senate had developed task forces to try to figure out what was going on. The many families that were dealing with the loss of their loved ones had pushed and pushed and pushed to try to shine a light on the issue and solve these crimes.

The local paper, the *Yakima Herald-Republic*, had run well over a dozen stories on the problem during the past year, but even with the stories, the task forces, and money sent by the federal government, it seemed the authorities were no closer to figuring out what might be happening. The case of Emily Pinkham was just the most recent of these mysterious deaths and disappearances, and it stoked the flames of the rumors that there was a serial killer out there who preyed on Native women.

Not all cities the size of Yakima had an FBI office. But because the Confederated Tribes and Bands of the Yakama Nation was one of the largest Native American tribes in the West, they often called the FBI in to help with criminal investigations. The FBI had been working hand-in-hand with Yakama Nation police on the cases of murdered and missing women, and after the discovery of the woman's identity, the FBI agent out of the Yakima office called a meeting in Toppenish of the various law enforcement agencies to discuss the death and discovery of Pinkham.

FBI special agent Sara Sinclair was new to the local office. She'd been working in Yakima since the first of the year and had spent the past four months getting up to speed on the investigation. The discovery of Pinkham's body was the first new case on her desk as a potential victim of a possible serial killer.

Sinclair had previously worked in the field office in Portland, but when the last agent in Yakima took a job in Washington D.C., she had applied for the transfer and gotten it. She was somewhat familiar with the case of the growing number of missing and murdered Native women and wanted to see if she could help solve them. And she had. Or at least, she had solved a couple. Her work had helped locate two different missing women. One was found living in a homeless encampment outside of Boise, and another was located with relatives in Eastern Montana.

The woman in Montana had left after her habitually-abusive husband had smacked her around in another drunken rage. When he'd finally passed out she had taken a Seattle Mariners souvenir baseball bat and had whacked him about the head and body. She didn't care if he was dead. She jumped in their Nissan Pathfinder and headed east until she ran out of gas money.

The husband didn't die, but he did have a cracked skull, a couple broken ribs, and hurt like hell for a few weeks. As he recovered from his injuries he thought maybe he'd been lucky to escape death, and didn't care if he ever saw his wife again.

The woman's relatives in Wapato had reported her missing, and although the Yakama Tribal police suspected the man of possibly killing his wife, with no body or other real evidence, they didn't have enough to press charges. Still, her name had been added to the list of mysterious disappearances, that is until Sinclair had located her.

She had done other work around the region too, including some drug trading investigations with the DEA and a possible human trafficking case, but most of her time was spent on cases within the boundaries of the 1,130,000 acres of the Yakama Nation reservation.

Sinclair was a fit, five-foot, ten-inch woman, with straight black hair cut to her shoulders. When McCain saw her walk into the meeting room, he thought she looked a little like the actress who played the medical examiner in the first *Men in Black* movie.

He couldn't come up with the actress's name at the moment, but he'd think of it.

McCain and Hargraves had been invited to the meeting because they'd been involved in the bear investigation that ultimately led to Pinkham's body. Also in attendance were Yakima County Sheriff's deputies Williams, Garcia and Stratford, as well as a couple of State Patrol officers, and three Yakama Nation police officers.

After a quick around-the-room introduction of all the attendees, Sinclair said, "Here's what we know: Miss Pinkham went missing on or about November 15th, and she was found on April 1. In that time no other Native women have gone missing, nor have any been murdered. That is the good news. But there are still at least seventeen cases that are open and unsolved from as far back as 2004."

Sinclair went on to discuss several of the other cases and mentioned that the woman McCain had found was the only one discovered in the Cascades, off the reservation. There were a few other anomalies as well, but still, because Pinkham had been Native American, Sinclair was including her in the group of missing women.

When the meeting was over, McCain and Hargraves went up to where Sinclair was putting papers in her briefcase and introduced themselves.

"Thanks for coming today, gentlemen," she said to them. "I appreciate your time and I've been looking forward to meeting you. I'd especially like to spend a few minutes discussing how you found the body, Mr. McCain."

"Sure," McCain said. "But there's probably not much more I can give you that wasn't in my report. We're not really part of this investigation, but we're happy to assist. That is, if we're not out running down lawless trout fishermen and such."

McCain and every other fish and wildlife officer knew that they were looked down upon somewhat by some members of the other police agencies. In their daily duties, rarely did they run across the really violent criminals like other officers did. Still, there was that whole deal about how most of the people they contacted were armed in some manner.

"Who's going to stop the perp who is catching a couple bass over their limit, if not you?" she asked, smiling at McCain. "We can definitely sleep better knowing you are out there protecting the perch."

McCain and Hargraves both chuckled.

Good looking *and* a sense of humor, McCain thought to himself. He didn't dare say that, what with everything going on in today's "Me Too" world. But he also thought if he had, she wouldn't have been bothered in the least.

"I can fill you in on the day we found the body now if you'd like, Agent Sinclair," McCain said. "Or we can meet at some other time to go over it."

"First of all, please call me Sara," she said. "When we're in formal settings we can do the whole agent thing, but in these private meetings let's keep it to first names. Okay with you guys?"

Hargraves and McCain agreed.

"I have to run to a phone conference with my boss and some big wigs at the Bureau of Indian Affairs," she said. "Give me your number and we'll catch up later."

The two WDFW officers gave Sinclair their cards with their cell numbers, and she gave them hers. And like that she was running out the door.

"Where has she been all my life?" Hargraves said to McCain.

"Well, she was probably in kindergarten about the time you and Linda were getting married," McCain said. "What would she want with an old, fat, married guy like you anyway?"

"Yeah, well, there is that," Hargraves said. "Now you on the other hand, you're not married, and got no one in your life except that yellow dog. I smell opportunity."

"We just met the woman. You think we can just cool it for a bit? Speaking of Jack, I gotta get home before he thinks he's been left for good and is going to starve to death."

It took McCain about twenty minutes to reach his little three-bedroom rambler that sat between Highway 12 and the Naches River near the town of Gleed. When he arrived, Jack was definitely ready to eat. He jumped up and down and barked with excitement in the backyard where he spent the days when he wasn't on patrol with McCain.

"Oh, for crying out loud," McCain said to the yellow dog. "I'm only a half hour late. I think you're going to live."

McCain liked living out in the country. He had grown up in the country, and after living in a neighborhood in Mill Creek on his last assignments with the WDFW where the houses were so close you could run and jump from one roof to the next, he made a promise to himself that wherever he landed next, he was going to get out of the city.

Frankly, the house wasn't much. About 1600 square feet, built in the 1960s, it wasn't fancy by any means. But as a single man, with only a spoiled dog to care for, the house was just perfect. There was a lawn that needed mowing weekly during half the year, and there was a patch of dirt in the back of the yard where McCain had had ambitious plans for growing some vegetables.

The garden hadn't worked out, as McCain kept falling further behind on the weeding. Pretty soon, you couldn't see the cucumber plants from all the thistles and other weeds. Williams and his wife had come over for a little backyard barbecue not long after he had planted the garden, and the deputy just looked at it and laughed.

"What are you growing in there?" he asked.

"I planted some tomatoes, cucumbers, and some sweet corn," McCain told him proudly.

"Why would you do that to yourself?" Williams asked. "Don't you know you can run down to one of the produce stands in the Lower Valley and get all the vegetables you want for ten bucks."

As it turned out, Williams was right, of course. The farmers in the Lower Valley were excellent at growing row crops, and for just a few bucks, you could have fresh-grown veggies, sweet corn and melons all summer long. Best of all, you didn't have to hoe one row or pull one weed.

McCain fed Jack and fixed himself a ham sandwich. Like the dog, McCain ate quickly. Then he called Jack, and the two were off to the river.

Being within walking distance of the Naches River was another reason he liked living where he did. His road led to a public access to the river, and many evenings during the summer he and Jack would walk down there and fish for trout. During the spring, when the river was closed to fishing, McCain still enjoyed spending time along the stream. McCain would work with Jack on his retrieving and commands, and McCain would spend time thinking about things as he watched and listened to the river roll along.

When he and Jack made it to the river, he wasn't surprised when a mule deer doe and last year's fawn jumped out of some wild roses. The deer bounced a couple of times and then stopped and stared at him and the dog.

Many people didn't realize just how many deer lived this close to town year-round. McCain had even seen elk in the trees along the river a few times. McCain thought it was a shame that people rushed by on the freeway day-in and day-out and never saw the wildlife that lived along the river corridor.

As they walked along the stream, McCain threw a retrieving dummy for Jack to fetch. He threw it into the river and, after giving the dog the command to fetch, Jack leaped from the bank, flying through the air. The dog splashed down hard, almost dunking his head, before he swam to the dummy that was rapidly floating downstream with the current. Jack was a strong swimmer and had the dummy back to McCain in no time. Then, for a change of pace, McCain threw the dummy into a big clump of brush. Jack, not-so-patiently but obediently, sat by McCain's side until he gave the command to fetch. When he heard his name, the big yellow dog tore off toward the brush and searched hard until he found the dummy. As with just about every other Labrador retriever McCain had ever known, Jack loved to play fetch.

As they played and walked, McCain thought about meeting the new FBI agent. Sara Sinclair was definitely attractive. Hargraves had that right. And she was obviously smart. McCain hadn't seen a wedding ring on her finger, but that didn't mean she wasn't in a relationship.

After a couple major catastrophes in his love life, McCain was more than a little gun-shy about jumping into another relationship any time soon. But a woman like Sinclair, well, he thought that just might change his mind about trying it again.

He was thinking about the FBI agent when he heard the whistling of wood ducks from above. He searched the skies and saw a pair of the beautiful ducks swing overhead and settle into a slow spot in the river across from them. McCain looked at Jack, and the dog was at full alert. He'd heard and seen the ducks too, and was now quivering in anticipation, waiting for McCain to tell him to fetch the birds.

"Settle down," McCain said to the dog. "We won't be hunting ducks for another six months."

He told the dog to come, and they continued their walk up the river. Along the way they jumped a small flock of mallards and a pair of Canada geese, and when McCain noticed that Jack had stopped and was looking intently at something across the river, he saw a mink slinking along the water's edge

"Good eyes there, mister," McCain said to Jack, who ignored the comment and watched the little animal as it searched along the riverbank for a crawdad or something else to eat.

He threw the dummy a few more times for Jack and thought about the woman they had found in the mountains. How did she die and why was she there? As the investigation progressed, he wondered if he'd get to spend more time working with Sara Sinclair. He smiled at the prospect. He definitely hoped so.

CHAPTER 5

A second woman's body was discovered in the Cascades west of Yakima in mid-May. A young couple hunting shed antlers with their dogs had discovered the remains at the edge of a small meadow.

Every spring as the weather warms and the snowline recedes, people head into the woods looking for deer and elk antlers that had been shed by the bucks and bulls in January, February and March. While deer antlers are always gladly scooped up, it is the much larger elk antlers that are the real trophies of the shed hunters.

Some shed hunters use looking for them as an excuse to be in the mountains, getting some good exercise and fresh air, while others are in it strictly for the money. There is a good market for shed antlers as buyers will resell them into some of the Asian markets. There the antlers are ground down and used for medicinal purposes. Antlers have been used for over 2,000 years in China, where they are believed to strengthen bones and muscles, benefit the kidneys and spleen, and promote blood flow.

McCain had been called out several times in the past few years when reports came in that shed hunters were jumping the elk fences on state lands. They came in under the cover of darkness to be the first to check out the lands near the WDFW elk feeding stations. He figured there must really be some good money in selling the sheds, as he had ticketed one guy three times for trespassing after he had entered the closed areas looking for sheds. McCain thought the man must just factor in a $158 fine once or twice as part of the cost of doing business.

The shed hunters who had discovered the body were legal shed hunters, and they were admittedly new to the sport. Chris Avery and his girlfriend, Mandy Spiers, were enjoying the beautiful spring day with their two golden retrievers, Mutt and Jeff, when the dogs started paying particular attention to some brush near a meadow. Even though the dogs were not trained to locate sheds, Avery was hoping that maybe a big bull elk had not made it through winter and the dogs were attracted to the decaying flesh of a dead animal.

As he got closer, Avery could see he was right, at least about the dogs being attracted to something dead. Unfortunately, what they were attracted to was definitely not an elk.

The man thought he was going to lose his lunch when he saw the bloody human remains in the grass. His girlfriend wasn't so lucky. In one big eruption she lost every bit of the nice little picnic lunch she had enjoyed while sitting on a blanket not an hour before.

McCain didn't normally get non-wildlife calls, but based on where the body had been found, and how it might have some similarities to the body Jack had tracked, dispatch called.

"What's your location?" the dispatcher asked.

"I'm out past Selah talking to some folks about a possible wolf sighting," he answered.

"Another body has been found in the mountains," the dispatcher said. "Looks like another woman. YSO would like you to come up if you have the time."

"Text me the location and I'll roll right away," McCain said.

McCain couldn't believe it. He'd been working out of the Region 3 office for nine years and only two times before had he been involved in a call with a dead body. One of the prior calls had been to help locate a fisherman who had capsized his drift boat after getting caught by a sweeper on the upper Yakima River and had drowned. The other was a homeless guy who had been living on an island in the lower river. Now, in the span of two months here he was headed to another body discovered in the Cascades.

McCain hopped on Wenas Road and headed northwest. He went by a new housing development being built in what were alfalfa fields just a few years before and continued past Wenas Lake to where the pavement ended and three unpaved roads split in three directions. He stayed on the left road, veered left again when it forked, and got on a smaller dirt road that followed Milk Canyon up to the top of Cleman Mountain.

According to dispatch, the kids who had found the body were just northeast of the old Cleman Mountain lookout. Within a few minutes, McCain spotted two Yakima sheriff's rigs and a silver Toyota Tacoma parked in the sagebrush just off the road. He couldn't see anyone but knew the deputies couldn't be too far, so he pulled over and parked next to the other rigs.

He climbed out, let Jack out, and looked around for the group's tracks. It didn't take long. Four people can trample up some ground without much effort, and McCain was soon able to distinguish at least one of the tracks. Williams had fairly large feet for a man just six feet in height, and from working with the deputy on several other cases, he knew Williams wore a good-sized boot.

Interestingly, there was a second track, with a different sole than the boots Williams wore—at least a size 12, maybe bigger. McCain had no idea if they were the tracks of the young man who had been up here looking for shed antlers or the other deputy who had come on the call. The fourth set of tracks was much smaller, obviously those of the young woman shed hunter.

"C'mon, Jack," McCain said to the yellow dog, and off they went following the trail of boot tracks made in the arid soil.

They followed the tracks up a hill for about a half mile, through scattered pine trees and buck brush, and then cut over a small ridge to the north. When they crested the hill, Jack's ears went up, and McCain knew he had heard the voices from the people at the body.

"Okay," McCain said to the dog. "Go find them."

Jack took off on a run, with McCain trying to follow as quickly as he could without twisting an ankle on the rocks, or worse yet, breaking a leg.

He heard Williams's voice in the distance say, "Hey Jack! Where's that no-good partner of yours?"

"I'm right here," McCain said as he came around a small growth of young pine trees. "But I'm not sure why. This is YSO's call from what I can tell."

Actually, McCain was glad he had been asked to come take a look. He wanted to see if there were any similarities to the body of the Pinkham woman other than the fact that it had been found on the east side of the Cascades, miles and miles from anywhere.

McCain said his hellos to Williams and the young deputy Stratford and introduced himself to the two antler hunters. Jack did the sniffing-to-get-to-know-you routine all dogs do with Mutt and Jeff. Within twenty seconds the three dogs were romping up the hill, chasing each other with tails wagging a hundred miles an hour.

"What a beautiful dog," the young lady said to McCain. "Deputy Stratford here says he's a tracking dog. Did he track us here?"

"No," McCain said. "I followed your tracks. Williams here leaves a print like Sasquatch, and evidently . . ." McCain paused and looked at the feet of the other two men, "so does Stratford. Both size 12 or 13 if I'm not mistaken."

McCain looked more closely at the young female shed hunter. She was white as a sheet and was nursing a bottle of water like it was a gift from God.

Something, probably coyotes, with the help of ravens and magpies, had made a mess of the body. The woman's eyes were missing, and the body had literally been torn apart and mostly eaten from the inside out. Like that of the Native woman found earlier, this woman had long black hair. But there were no other distinguishing marks or clues that might tell if she, too, had been Native American. She definitely could have been, but she also could have been of Mexican or Central American descent, or a white woman with black hair.

McCain looked closely at the body and concentrated on the chest area. He knew how scavengers fed. They would get into the main body cavity to eat the organs first. He couldn't be certain, because the body had been ravaged, but it looked like the chest of this woman had been partially sliced open. McCain recalled the body of the other woman and remembered thinking that her torso might have been cut open prior to being scavenged as well.

The county coroner had found no clear cause for death of the Pinkham woman, and it was McCain's opinion he would have trouble determining a cause of death for this woman too. The coyotes and birds had pretty much made sure of that.

"The crime lab folks are on their way," Williams said. "And dispatch said the FBI agent wants to see the body before it is moved."

"A regular alphabet soup of investigators," Stratford said. "YSO, WDFW, FBI."

Williams just looked at the young deputy and then back to McCain and said, "So, any thoughts McCain?"

"Not really," McCain said.

"I'm guessing this was a hiker who got lost and succumbed to the elements," Stratford said.

"Could be," Williams said. "But you don't see many women hikers out here on their own."

"My friend Ashley goes hiking by herself all the time," said the very pale Mandy Spiers. "She hikes all over these mountains. She's like that woman who hiked the Pacific Crest Trail from Mexico to Canada. You know the one they made the movie about that starred Reese Witherspoon."

McCain felt like asking if her friend had long black hair but refrained.

"Well, I've seen all I need to see," said McCain. "Why don't you folks hike back to the rigs with me and Jack and leave the deputies here to do their job?"

He whistled for Jack, who came back with the two golden retrievers in tow, and McCain and the shed hunters and the three dogs headed up over the ridge toward the vehicles.

CHAPTER 6

McCain had driven most of the way down the mountain when his phone rang.

"This is McCain," he said into the cab of the truck.

"Officer McCain, this is Agent Sinclair. We met the other day at the meeting down in Toppenish."

"Yes, Agent Sinclair," McCain said. "How may I help you?"

He wondered what happened to all the crap about keeping things on a first name basis, but he guessed this was official business.

"I hear you're up at the body of a woman that some people found in the mountains."

"I *was* up there," he said. "But I'm on my way back down to town."

"Any chance you'd be interested in going back up there?" she asked. "I'd like to see the body for myself, before it's transported to the morgue."

"Sure, but you'll have to ride along with my yellow Lab, Jack," McCain explained. "He's not too much of a bother. Where are you right now?"

"I'm on I-82, just passing the Selah exit."

"Okay, get off on the next exit, get on North Wenas Road and follow it all the way north until you leave the pavement. I'll be waiting for you there. I'll be in the tan Ford F-150 with a yellow dog sticking his head out the window."

"See you soon," the FBI agent said. "Oh, and by the way, I love dogs."

Agent Sinclair showed up in a black Chrysler that screamed law enforcement. McCain figured that driving those cars was mandated as part of the purchase plan by the federal government back when some of the car companies were failing.

"Do they make you drive that rig?" McCain asked as Sinclair walked up to him where he sat on the tailgate of the pickup. "Or did you choose that one out of the motor pool?"

The image of the dark-haired agent in the black rig again reminded him of the actress in the *Men in Black* movie. What was that lady's name?

"Hey, I like this car," she said. "It's got plenty of power and, while the gas mileage sucks, I can get to where I want to be plenty fast."

"Well, they will see you coming from six miles away," McCain said.

"And they can't see you coming with that giant badge on the doors and the extra-large radio antenna on the roof?" Agent Sinclair extended her hand, and said, "Thanks Luke, I really appreciate it. Now where is this dog I've heard so much about?"

Oh, so now we ARE on a first name basis, McCain thought to himself. He was okay with that.

The last time McCain had seen Jack he was tearing around a giant ponderosa, hot on the heels of a gray squirrel. He whistled, and a moment later Jack came running up a dry creek bed, tail wagging and tongue dragging.

"He looks like he's having a good time," Sinclair said.

Jack came over to the person who had magically appeared

while he was off chasing the forest creatures. He sniffed Sinclair, and then he let her scratch his ears.

"Okay, you've passed the Jack test," McCain said. "Anyone who is okay by him is okay by me. Let's load up. We're burning daylight."

On the jarring ride back up the road, Sinclair started peppering him with questions. Since they hadn't had a chance to talk about the discovery of the first woman's body, she asked him to give her all the details. He started at the beginning, telling of the bear hunters shooting and field dressing the bear, finding the ear and then leading the deputies and WDFW officers to the bear. He then told how he put Jack on the trail, backtracking the bear until they had discovered the body.

She asked him about seventy-three more questions, and McCain answered every one patiently and with as much detail as he could. Her questions were thoughtful and smart, and he was impressed with how she was seemingly thinking everything through.

When they arrived back at the place where he had parked earlier, there was just one YSO rig remaining. And when they made it back over the hill to where the body was found, they discovered that Deputy Stratford had been assigned the duty of hanging out at the crime scene to keep the birds and any other scavengers away until the crime scene folks arrived. Stratford was sitting twenty yards or so from the remains, looking at his cell phone.

"You remember Agent Sinclair from the meeting the other day?" he asked Stratford as they walked down the hill toward him.

"Yes, I do," Stratford said. "I'm looking forward to hearing your take on all of this."

With that, Sinclair started looking closely at the gruesome mess that, at some point in time, had been a healthy woman. She took photos with her cell phone, some up close, others farther away. And, with an extending wand-type apparatus that she magically pulled out of her pocket, she poked and probed different areas of the bones and meat. She didn't say a word.

When she was done, she looked at McCain and said, "Okay, we can head back now."

McCain looked at Stratford, who looked back at McCain, and then they both turned and watched as Sinclair marched up the hill.

"Not one for a lot of questions or small talk," Stratford said.

"You should ride up a bumpy road with her," McCain said. "I'm her lift outta here, so I guess I better catch up. The crime scene people should be here shortly."

And with that he gave the deputy a head nod, turned, whistled for Jack, and headed up the trail after Sinclair.

When they got back to the truck the guys with the State Patrol crime lab were just unloading a stretcher and other equipment. McCain showed them the now obvious trail to the body that was getting worn into the grass and dirt and wished them good luck.

Back in the truck, bumping down the two-track road, Sinclair turned to McCain and asked him what he thought about the discovery of the woman's body.

"What do you think?" Sinclair asked.

"Well, I don't think she was a lost hiker," McCain said. "And, she wasn't up here looking for mushrooms or antlers. The clothing is just not right. I think she was killed someplace else and dropped out here. Looking at the surroundings there were no signs of a struggle, and while there was some blood, there should have been more under the body."

"That's what I thought too," Sinclair said. "And, I don't think this woman was Native American."

"Well, I guess that's good, huh?" McCain said.

"Why would someone bring a body way up here?" she asked, almost to herself.

"Think about it," McCain said. "It's the perfect place to get rid of a body without being seen. And if someone does find the remains, they will most likely be a bleached-out bunch of bones scattered in nine directions."

"Yeah, except for the two bodies that have been found recently. They weren't a bunch of bones."

"They weren't too far from it," McCain said. "Give them a couple more months, after the bones had been picked clean by the crows and magpies, and the summer sun had pounded away at them. Then they'd be hard to distinguish from any other animal's bones out here."

"Hmmm," thought Sinclair.

"There could be a dozen other women's bodies out here if someone has been doing this for a while," McCain said.

"Or more," Sinclair said.

They got back to Sinclair's super sedan, and as she was climbing out of McCain's truck, she said, "I haven't eaten anything since I had a really bad energy bar at eleven. You want to go grab a bite someplace?"

About that time McCain's stomach growled loud enough that both Sinclair and Jack turned and looked at him.

"I guess I could eat," McCain said. "I know a great little pizza place that also has sandwiches and salads."

"I was thinking more along the lines of a steak and a baked potato," she said. "But okay, if you need a salad to keep up your boyish figure, I'm good with that."

"I have to drop Jack at home and feed him. How about we meet in a half hour?"

"Sounds fine. Give me the directions to the pizza place."

Over dinner they talked mostly about the two bodies in the mountains and about work in general. He was surprised that Sinclair was so interested in his work and wanted to know how he had trained Jack to be a tracker. Of course, McCain hadn't really done much training. Jack was a natural, and McCain had just allowed his abilities to come out.

They talked a little about their personal lives too. Sinclair had been raised in Northern California and had gotten her law degree from the University of Oregon before joining the FBI. He teased her about being a Duck, and when she learned he had graduated from Washington State University she razzed him to no end about how Oregon had been beating WSU like a rented mule in just about every sport there was.

"Hey!" McCain said defensively. "We beat Oregon in field hockey last year."

"Field hockey!" she snorted. "Is that even a sanctioned sport?"

Later, as they walked out of the restaurant, McCain asked her if she had a coat hanger in her car.

"No, why?" she asked.

"Oh, I've heard you Oregon Ducks all keep a hanger in your car. You know, just in case you lock your keys in there too."

"What?" she asked. And then she burst out laughing.

That night, McCain had just gone to bed and was reading the latest issue of *Western Hunting Journal* when his phone buzzed. It was a text and it read: *Did you hear about the WSU student who was two hours late to class? Evidently, the power went out and he got stuck on an escalator.*

McCain smiled and went back to an article about hunting snow cocks in Nevada. He was going to do that someday. He wondered if Jack could handle the tough terrain and extremely high elevations. Then he thought, "To heck with Jack, I wonder if I can handle them."

The next morning, with the possibility of hiking the craggy peaks of the White Mountains of Nevada fresh on his mind, McCain went extra hard during his workout. Jack, well, he just lay on McCain's bed and watched.

CHAPTER 7

The next week of work was going by quickly. He'd had to appear in court for a couple of poaching cases that he and Hargraves had worked together. One involved a father-son duo who had decided they wanted to get into the bear bladder business and had set up several bear-baiting sites up in the Ahtanum, west of Yakima. A disgruntled hunter had come upon two of the illegal baits and had informed the folks in the WDFW office about it.

Hargraves and McCain had taken turns sitting on the sites, and after a couple days, in wandered one LeRoy Johnson Jr. Short, at about five foot seven, overweight by thirty pounds and slightly balding, Johnson had arrived with a rifle and set up in a ground blind that had been placed near a fifty-gallon drum baited with apples, week-old donuts and used French fry oil.

When Hargraves had enough video of the man checking out the drum and sitting in the blind with his rifle pointed out the window, he went over and had a little chat with him.

"Can I see your hunting license and bear tag?" Hargraves asked the potential poacher.

"I got a license, but no tag," the man said. "I used my tag already."

"I see," said Hargraves. "You realize that you can only shoot one bear a year, and it is against the law to keep hunting bears after you've filled your tag?"

"Yeah, but Daddy said I needed to keep coming out here. I shot three bears so far, and Daddy, he's shot four."

Upon hearing that, Hargraves asked to see Johnson's rifle, placed handcuffs on the man, and escorted him back to his truck. As Hargraves took the younger Johnson back down toward town, he radioed McCain, and after telling him about the situation, asked him to meet him at the Johnson's house in Tieton.

"You might wait out of sight until I get there," Hargraves said. "We wouldn't want to tip off the old man and have him start hiding bear parts under the house or anything."

"Roger that," McCain replied.

As it was, the old man had already hidden a bunch of the parts around their twenty-acre property. He denied having shot any more bears than the one he was allowed and called his son an idiot.

LeRoy Johnson, Sr. was a carbon copy of his son. Or technically, the younger Johnson was a carbon copy of the old man. He had the same round face, thinning hair, and was roughly the same height as his son but not carrying as much weight. He wore blue overalls, a striped logger's shirt with the sleeves torn off and a trucker style cap that said "PETA—People Eating Tasty Animals" above the bill.

"You can tell that Junior weren't blessed with a whole lotta brains," he said. "He likes to hunt, so I let him."

"So you don't mind us looking around then?" Hargraves asked the elder Johnson.

He told the officers he had no problem with that, and after they found nine freshly severed bear paws in the garage, one over the two-bear limit unless one of the Johnsons had shot a five-legged bear, they decided to bring Jack in to do some sniffing around. By the time the yellow dog had searched the entire property they found evidence, by way of five bear skulls, buried here and there. With the two that the Johnsons claimed they took legally, that made seven, just like Junior had said.

"He may not be the sharpest hook in the tackle box," Hargraves said to McCain, "but he does know how to add up dead bears."

It turned out Johnson Sr. had been selling the bladders and other bear parts to a buyer who was selling the stuff on the black market. Like deer antlers, bear parts were a hot commodity, used in different areas of the world for medicinal purposes. The last McCain had heard, a bladder was worth about $1,500 to the person selling it to the black-market traders. The Johnsons had made over ten grand with their little poaching enterprise.

As he sat in court, waiting to testify in the case of the State of Washington versus LeRoy Johnson Sr. and LeRoy Johnson Jr., McCain typed out a text: *Did you hear about the Oregon Duck who won a gold medal at the Olympics? He liked it so much he had it bronzed.* McCain added a little smiley face emoji and pushed send.

The Johnsons were found guilty. They both lost their hunting rights for five years. They also had all the rifles in their possession confiscated, and each received a $5,000 fine. Finally, Johnson Sr., as the ringleader of the two-man operation, was sentenced to nine months in jail to begin serving immediately.

A few days later, McCain was doing an early morning check on some anglers down at a couple of the popular gravel pit fishing ponds along I-82 near Donald when he got a call on the radio.

"Can you get up to the county jail as soon as possible?" the dispatcher asked.

"10-4," McCain responded. "What's up?"

"There's been a jail break," the dispatcher said. "They are asking for help from WDFW."

When McCain arrived, he counted thirteen cop cars, light bars lit up like a Christmas tree, parked this way and that on the streets around the jail. He pulled up next to the local ABC television van and recognized one of the young reporters he'd watched on the early evening news.

The reporter looked like he was barely old enough to have graduated from high school, and although it was a bit hard to detect, he had a slight speech impediment. The news director must have really liked the kid though, because he was the go-to guy for live reports whenever news was breaking.

As McCain walked by the reporter, he heard him say, "Hi, dis is Simon Erickson, reporting live from da Yakima County jail, where I am toad seventeen prisoners escaped from da jail in da early morning hours."

McCain just kept on walking looking for Williams or someone who could tell him what had happened and why he might be needed. As he walked, he wondered if Simon Erickson had graduated from WSU's school of journalism. If so, he sure hoped Sinclair didn't find out.

Ultimately, he found the director of the county jail, one Robert Dyson, who gave him a brief situation report. Dyson was a gruff-looking man of about sixty. He had big bushy eyebrows and a five o'clock shadow, even though it was just 9:30 in the morning. The man, McCain thought, looked like he was tougher than a boiled owl, and would take no guff from anyone.

According to Dyson, a group of inmates decided they'd had enough of incarceration, broken a table in two, and used one half to jam up entry into the lower level exercise area. They then used the other half of the table as a battering ram and had broken open a door to the outside. At that point all they had to do was jump the ten-foot-high spiked fence and they were free as the birds.

According to an early morning jogger who was running by about the time the door busted open, it looked like a bunch of bees boiling out of a hive. He said the inmates ran out the door, jumped the fence and scattered like a covey of quail.

In all, seventeen inmates had escaped before jail enforcement officers could get the door closed and things secure. Reporter Erickson had been correct in that. McCain wondered why, if there were seventeen inmates on the loose, all the law enforcement folks were crowded around the jail. They should be out looking for a bunch of dudes in orange jump suits.

"One of the escapees was a LeRoy Johnson Sr.," Dyson said, looking through his bushy eyebrows at McCain. "I understand you've had some dealings with him."

"Yes sir," McCain said. "We caught him and his son, LeRoy Johnson Jr. poaching bears a couple months ago up in the national forest west of town. He's just a few days in on a nine-month sentence."

"Well, evidently jail didn't suit him much," Dyson said. "Our videos show that he was one of the instigators of our little jail break. YPD and YSO have already rounded up nine of the inmates, but with eight on the loose, including Johnson, we could use some help. It is our guess that Mr. Johnson may have had a vehicle or a ride waiting for him, and he could be who-knows-where by now."

McCain said he would do some checking out at Johnson's place and talk to LeRoy Junior to see what he could find out. As he walked back to his truck, he saw that the young ABC reporter was now talking to a skinny man with wild, curly black hair wearing a black Adidas sweat suit and a bandana tied around his head.

"Dis is Mr. Carl Whitehead, who witnessed da escape. Tell us, what did you see dis morning?" Simon asked as he stuck a microphone into the jogger's face.

You gotta give the kid credit, McCain thought to himself as he loaded up and headed toward Tieton.

When McCain got out to the Johnson homestead he stopped at the entrance of the dirt driveway and took it all in. The place had a look of desertion. It hadn't been much to look at when the Johnsons were living there, but now it felt like a ghost town. There were still piles of junk here and there, along with a couple broken down cars, but it looked like no one had been home for a while. McCain recalled that when he and Hargraves had showed up the day they had arrested the Johnsons, he'd had to kick a whole herd of chickens out of the way just to walk up to the house. The chickens were gone. And so, evidently, was LeRoy Johnson Jr.

Dyson had told McCain to report to YSO Deputy Williams, so when he found no one around and the house basically deserted, he called Williams on his cell.

"Hey, Rifleman," Williams said. "Tell me you've found Mr. Johnson?"

"No can do," McCain said into the Bluetooth microphone. "The place is pretty much empty. They've even moved the chickens out. Can you check with Yakima and Kittitas County records to see if our friends own any land anywhere else around here?"

"Will do," said Williams. "I'll get back to you ASAP."

With that Williams clicked off, and McCain headed back to the office.

A couple hours later McCain's phone buzzed, and he saw Williams was calling back.

McCain answered and said, "Find anything?"

"Well, records don't show any other properties owned by LeRoy Johnson, senior or junior. But there is a cabin up out of Cle Elum, owned by a Theodore Johnson. Now, I know there are like a million Johnsons in the state, but this Johnson's previous driver's license showed the same Tieton address as LeRoy one and LeRoy two."

"Interesting. Maybe another son of LeRoy Senior, or maybe a brother?"

"Could be either," Williams said. "But looking at his age, it most likely is another son. And by the driver's license photo of Theodore, you can see they've definitely been kicked by the same mule."

"Okay," McCain said. "I'm going to go grab Jack and then head up there. Text me the address."

CHAPTER 8

Cle Elum was an old mining town in Kittitas County, just off Interstate 90 between Ellensburg and the summit of Snoqualmie Pass. It was a nice community, located in the coniferous forest in the mid-elevations of the Cascades. The little town had seen considerable growth over the past fifteen years, as more and more people from Seattle moved to the area and commuted an hour and a half each way to jobs at Microsoft, Starbucks and Amazon. The employees who bought stock in these companies early on had become multi-millionaires when their shares had soared in value. There were stories of Microsoft janitors who had scraped a few thousand dollars together to buy stock in those early days and were now living in palatial homes around Seattle. Some of the employees or former employees, lived in beautiful million-dollar homes around a golf resort known as Suncadia in Cle Elum.

There were plenty of older homes and cabins scattered around the area too, and that was what McCain was looking at when he found the little cabin owned by Theodore Johnson. He stopped well short of the driveway to the cabin and parked, leaving Jack in the truck. He walked through a growth of small fir trees to see what he could see of the cabin. The tiny cabin was set off the road a good 300 yards and surrounded by mature firs and pine trees. McCain could see a little smoke rolling out of the chimney and three pickups parked out front.

He recognized the pickup owned by LeRoy Junior. He had seen the truck at the Johnson's place. The other two trucks he didn't recognize. He went back to his rig and called Williams.

"I've got three trucks," McCain said. "All pickups. One Chevy that I know is LeRoy Junior's, but the other two, both Dodge Rams, I haven't seen. I'll text you the license plates if you could run them for me. And, if there are three or more guys up here, I wouldn't mind a little support. I have Jack, but another officer would make me feel a little more warm and fuzzy inside."

"Roger that," Williams said. "I'll call Kittitas County and see if they have a deputy in the area."

McCain had a computer in his truck and had run about 27,000 plates in his life, but he didn't want to be sitting there watching a computer screen when he could be keeping an eye on the Johnson clan. Instead he texted the two license plates to Williams.

In case he needed to defend himself, his truck was outfitted with a Springfield Armory .223 rifle with a suppressor and a Remington 870 12-gauge shotgun. Both long guns sat in a special rack in the truck next to a catch pole which he occasionally used to keep snarling dogs at bay, or to help secure the odd deer that caught a leg in a barbed wire fence and needed saving. The shotgun was loaded with double aught buckshot and rifled slugs, placed alternately in the extended magazine.

McCain rarely used the shotgun, and only pulled the rifle when he needed to put down an injured elk or deer. He decided maybe he'd go ahead and grab the shotgun to carry along when heading into chat with the Johnsons. Even though he practiced at the range once a month with his service pistol, McCain was much more comfortable with a rifle or shotgun in his hands.

He was back in the little stand of firs watching the cabin when his phone buzzed. He checked the phone and saw a text from Williams. *Truck 2 owned by Theodore Johnson. Truck 3 owned by Aaron Armitage. Johnson has no priors but Armitage has done a little time at Coyote Ridge. Kittitas Co. deputy is three minutes out.* McCain texted *"Thx"* back at Williams and moved slowly back to his truck to await the Kittitas deputy.

The deputy pulled up next to McCain's truck, jumped out and introduced herself as Alivia Hernandez. She was about five foot four inches tall, and stout but definitely not fat. A couple of tattoos were peeking out of her shirtsleeves on her biceps.

"Whatta we got?" Hernandez asked.

McCain filled her in and told her he thought one of them should go in from the front and knock on the door, while the other watched the back to see who, if anyone, might come out that way.

"I'm not worried about any real problems," McCain said. "But in this situation, it is good to keep our bases covered."

It was decided that Hernandez would go in and knock on the front door, and McCain would swing around with Jack and watch the back.

When Hernandez tapped on the door, a voice from inside said, "Who is it?"

"Kittitas County Sheriff," Hernandez hollered. "Can you please come to the door?"

A man opened the main wooden door, peered through the screen door and asked, "What do you want?"

"Are you Theodore Johnson?" Hernandez asked the man who was just a few inches taller than her, with a round face and thinning hair.

"Yeah, I'm Teddy Johnson," the man said. "What can I do for you?"

"Mr. Johnson, you've probably heard there was a jail break down in Yakima this morning and your father was one of the inmates who jumped the fence. Any idea where we might find him?"

Johnson smiled at Hernandez and said, "No officer, I got no clue where he is. My brother LeRoy is here with me, but we ain't seen hide nor hair of the old man."

"Anyone else in there with you?" Hernandez asked.

"Yeah, my buddy Aaron's here, but that's it."

"So, you've not heard from your father today?"

"Me and the old man don't get along too good."

"So, that's a no?"

"Yeah, I ain't heard nothin' from him."

"You mind if I come in and look around?"

"Yeah, I would mind. So, unless you got a warrant, maybe you should leave."

Hernandez could smell pot, and from the look in Teddy's eyes, he was pretty well baked. She would like to get a look around inside but knew it probably wasn't a good idea to push it.

"Okay, Teddy," she said as she held out a card. "If you do hear from your father, you'd be doing him a favor by calling our office. You, your brother, and your friend don't need a harboring-a-fugitive conviction on your records."

Johnson reached around the slightly opened screen door, took the card, smiled a goofy smile, and closed the wooden door on Hernandez.

McCain was still waiting in some tall brush behind the house when he saw a window in the back corner of the cabin slide open and a man's leg appear. The body attached to the leg was that of the newly escaped LeRoy Johnson Sr. He dropped to the ground and briskly strode toward McCain.

"Hello, LeRoy," McCain said as Johnson walked past him.

LeRoy all but jumped out of his skin before collecting himself and spinning around with a wild roundhouse swing at McCain. He missed and took off running.

McCain hated running down a suspect. He was fit and a good runner, but he always felt encumbered in his ballistic vest and hated how everything in his utility belt flapped around. Johnson only made it about fifteen yards before he was hit from behind by McCain who didn't hold back after the attempted roundhouse. Both men went down in a cloud of dust. With the aid of McCain's forearm, Johnson's face was ground into the dirt and pine needles. He made a sound like someone was letting the air out of a rubber raft.

Johnson continued to grunt and groan and then said, "Well, damn it to hell."

McCain got up, helped Johnson to his feet, and placed handcuffs on his wrists. It was then he realized that Jack was standing in front of the man growling with bared teeth. As McCain replayed the event in his mind, he remembered seeing Jack running next to him during the sprint to tackle Johnson.

"Good boy," McCain said to the growling dog.

"You wouldn't let that yellar dog bite me, wouldja?" Johnson asked.

"If you make another run for it, you can count on it," McCain said.

Hernandez, hearing the ruckus at the rear of the cabin, had come around quickly to see what was going on. She had her service pistol drawn but put it away when she saw McCain with Johnson in cuffs.

"You okay?" she asked.

"Yeah, we're good," McCain said. "What's the story with the rest of the Johnsons?"

He sat the senior Johnson down on a stump and told Jack to sit a few feet from the man. Then he walked over to the deputy so they could talk in private.

"They claimed to not have seen or heard from Mr. Johnson," she said. "Maybe I should go back and have a little chat with them."

"Good idea, but if you guys can spare another deputy, you might want to call in a back-up."

McCain was still not too sure that the younger Johnsons, or their friend with the prison record, were above a little violence, especially if it were three on one.

"I want to get Johnson Senior back to Yakima," he said as he walked back toward LeRoy who was giving Jack an evil stare.

McCain had left his shotgun leaned up against the pine tree when he played linebacker on Johnson, so he grabbed it, got Johnson by the arm, and headed to the truck. Hernandez followed along and radioed for assistance.

On his way back to Yakima, McCain dialed up Deputy Williams.

"Got him," McCain said when Williams answered. "We'll be back at the county lock-up in forty-five. Let Dyson know, and you might mention to him that maybe they should bolt those tables down in the jail. It might save some future headaches."

"They had maintenance crews doing just that this afternoon when I was there," Williams said. "I think we've got all but a couple of the inmates rounded up. The county is offering a thousand-dollar reward for information on the two guys still out there. Someone will drop a dime on them, and we'll have them soon."

Chapter 9

The county coroner released the identity of the second woman twelve days after her body had been discovered in the Cascades by the shed hunters. She was identified by dental records as a twenty-six-year-old Mexican national who had been working in one of the fruit warehouses in Yakima. Her name was Sonya Alverez. She had been reported missing on March 11th by her boyfriend. He said she had gone to work at the warehouse and apparently just disappeared.

As McCain had suspected, the young woman hadn't been a hiker, and her disappearance had been a total mystery to her boyfriend and friends.

When she'd been reported missing, Yakima Police had suspected that her boyfriend, a twenty-nine-year-old Javier Garcia, might be involved with her disappearance. But Garcia had been in California visiting family from March 4th until he returned home when he couldn't reach his girlfriend. According to his cell phone history, he had tried to call Alverez several times on March 9th and for several days following.

According to her employer, Alverez had been at work on the 8th, but hadn't shown up for work as scheduled on the 9th or

10th or beyond. After Garcia learned his girlfriend had missed work, something she never did, and hadn't been in contact with any of her friends or co-workers, he filed a missing person report with the Yakima Police Department.

When McCain saw the photo of Alverez in the paper the next morning, he took a good look at it. He realized that Alverez and the Native American woman, Emily Pinkham, were of two different ethnicities, but if you looked at the photo quickly, you might think the two women were sisters.

The next day McCain called Sinclair and asked if she wanted to grab a steak someplace after work.

"Are you asking me out on a date, Officer McCain? Or is this business?"

"Call it what you want," he said. "I know you're not investigating the death of the Alverez woman, but I would like to hear your thoughts on the subject."

"I'd be up for a steak," she told McCain. "I'll even buy you a beer."

"Yeah, I'm really not much of a beer drinker."

"Not a beer drinker!" she responded. "You live in the hop-growing capital of the world, and you went to one of the biggest beer-drinking universities in the country, and you don't drink beer?"

"Long story," McCain said. "I'll tell you all about it at dinner."

After they hung up, McCain sent her a text: *Why do Oregon graduates place their diplomas on the dashboard of their cars? So they can park in the handicapped spots.*

He immediately received an emoji of a yellow round happy face, flipping the bird.

They met at the Sea Galley in Union Gap, a restaurant famous for their "We Got Crab Legs" advertising. McCain had never checked, but it might have been one of the last Sea Galleys left in the country. And, even though it was mainly a fish place, they served a darned good steak. Both McCain and Sinclair ordered up ribeyes, with a baked spud, all the fixings, and a dinner salad. Sinclair ordered a Bale Breaker Pale Ale, brewed just down the road in Moxee, and McCain had a Coke.

"So, what are you a recovering alcoholic or something?" she asked.

"That's not very sensitive. What if I am?" She briefly looked apologetic, and then McCain laughed. "I just never developed a taste for the stuff. Kinda tastes like donkey piss to me."

She laughed. "Have you ever tasted donkey piss?"

"No, but if I did, I bet it would be bitter and bad tasting, just like beer. I'm not big on any alcohol really. Plus, alcoholism runs on both sides of my family, and I figured if I had the addictive gene, well, I didn't really want to risk it."

"Makes sense," she said.

As they ate their salads and steaks, she talked a little about her work on the missing and murdered Native women. He told her about the bear-poaching Johnsons and how he'd run down the old man and tackled him.

"Yeah, I saw the deal on the jailbreak on the news," she said. "Did they really break out using a table?"

"Evidently," McCain said. "I think they've got it fixed now. Did you see the photo of the Alverez woman they identified as the body we saw in the mountains?"

"I did," Sinclair said. "I was the first person the coroner called, and he emailed me her photo. In a way I was glad it wasn't another Native woman. Still, it looks like a murder, and if it is related to the woman you and Jack found, well, that's not good."

"Did you notice how much the two women looked alike?" he asked. "From the two photos I saw, they could have been sisters."

"I was thinking the same thing," she said.

"You know, I'm not telling you how to do your job or anything, but if it was me, and I was an FBI agent, with all kinds of resources and fancy computers and minions who could do research for me at the drop of a hat, I might take a look at other women, Native and not, missing from the area that fit that same age and hair color profile."

"Good thinking," Sinclair said. "I asked our research folks to do that very thing just this morning."

Because the two bodies found in the Cascades were in Yakima County, off the reservation, the investigation was solely under the jurisdiction of the Yakima County Sheriff's Office. Still, she said she was watching the case with interest.

"I am too," McCain said. "Now, what do you want for dessert?" When they finished with dessert Sinclair said she had to get going, as she still needed to finish up a report before morning.

"Thanks for dinner," she said as they walked out the restaurant door. "I'm buying next time."

The next morning before McCain and Jack headed out for the day, McCain heard his phone buzz. There was a text. *I really enjoyed our dinner last night. Thanks again.*

McCain was thinking how nice the dinner was too, and then his phone buzzed again. *But I wouldn't call it a date. I can't date a Cougar.* The text ended with a smiley face. McCain grinned.

He and Jack had just fired up the pickup when dispatch called him. Someone, the dispatcher told him, had phoned in a report of some anglers fishing with night crawlers in the Yakima River above Roza Dam. The anglers were camped in the Big Pines Campground. McCain radioed back and said he'd head that way

When he arrived at Big Pines there were several RVs set up in designated spaces, with a few tents scattered around. McCain always wondered why anyone would choose this place to camp. There were thirty campgrounds along the rivers up in the mountains, surrounded by lush, green forest. This place was mostly dry desert and sagebrush. Whatever the appeal was,

McCain didn't know, but the campground was almost always full in the summer.

The man who called in the report about the bait fishermen, a Dallas Grimes, had told the dispatcher he was in a small Coachman motorhome with maroon and gold accent stripes. McCain spotted the RV, pulled up in front, left the rig on with the AC running for Jack, and went to knock on the door.

The man must've been watching for him, because he was just opening the door when McCain stepped up to knock.

"Mr. Grimes?" McCain asked.

Grimes was an averaged-sized man, probably seventy-five, with not much hair and a little too much belly. As soon as McCain started talking to the man a little dust-mop-type dog started yapping.

"Shush, Millie!" the man yelled at the dog, and then turned to McCain. "Yes, I'm Grimes. The guys who were fishing illegally just left. They were in a rusty-brown Ford Bronco II. You know, one of those older smaller ones that were dangerous to drive and fell apart after about 60,000 miles."

"Mmmm-hmmm," McCain said and was just about to ask the gentleman which way they went when Grimes hollered at the barking mop-dog again.

"Millie, quiet! I know they were a piece of crap because I used to own one. Probably the worst vehicle Ford ever made. Well, except for the Pinto, and maybe the Maverick. And then there was the Escort."

The dog kept yapping.

"Millie, shut up!" the man yelled.

"Mr. Grimes," McCain asked. "Did you see which way the vehicle went?"

The man reached down to swat the dog, missed, and about fell over because Millie had turned and was sprinting back into the bowels of the motorhome.

"They went upriver," Grimes said pointing up the highway.

McCain thought seriously about asking the man why in the world he had camped there, but he decided it wasn't worth it. He thanked the gentleman for reporting the bait-fishermen and turned to walk back to his truck. In the background he could hear Millie yapping.

The upper Yakima River, between Yakima and Ellensburg, had become one of the West's premier trout fishing streams. Regulations on the river were changed back in the 1990s to make that part of the river, all the way up to the headwaters in the Cascades, a catch-and-release only fishery. Fishing with bait was made illegal—only barbless, single-hooked flies, and lures were allowed.

Once the regulations changed it didn't take long before word of the quality of Yakima trout reached the fly-fishing world, and anglers from all over came to sample some of it. The popularity of the Brad Pitt movie, *A River Runs Through It*, certainly helped, as about a third of the folks living around Puget Sound decided they'd like to stand in a river and fling a fly. Seattle was less than two hours away, and soon the Yakima River became *the* place for the folks on the west side of the Cascades to come fish. The high percentage of the anglers knew the regulations, but every once in a while there would be someone who didn't know the rules, or more likely, was just ignoring them.

McCain spotted the brown Ford Bronco II parked in a pull-out about three miles up from the Big Pines campground. He parked far enough away that he could get out and walk up to watch the anglers for a bit. Sure enough, Grimes was right. The three men were using night crawlers. McCain could see a belly-up trout on a stringer in the water next to one of the men.

He went back to his truck, grabbed his citation book, let Jack out, had the dog heel, and walked over to talk to the three men.

"Hi, fellas" McCain said. "Can I see your fishing licenses and IDs?"

The men jumped a bit when McCain spoke, and then they started talking to one another in a foreign language. McCain thought they were speaking Russian.

"Yes, please, officer," the youngest of the three men said. "We are fishing okay, no?"

"No, you are not fishing okay," McCain said. "I need to see your fishing licenses and your driver's licenses."

"Yes, no please, we get for you," the youngest man said. He spoke to the two other men in Russian, and they reached into their back pockets for their billfolds and started digging through them for their licenses.

Similar to other states in the country, there were many new Russian immigrants in Washington and a lot of them liked to fish. Unfortunately, there were some who bent the laws just a tad. And there were a few who not only bent the laws, they broke them into about a thousand pieces.

The men handed McCain their licenses. Everything seemed to be in order. McCain asked if they could understand English, and they all nodded their heads. McCain could see in their eyes that maybe the only one who actually could was the youngest, a Sergi Ivanonov, according to his driver's license.

The whole time McCain was talking, the three men were watching Jack. They looked like they would jump in the river if the dog moved a step toward them.

McCain explained to Ivanonov the rules regarding no bait, and not being able to keep any trout in this part of the river. Ivanonov seemed honestly perplexed. He told them they needed to be sure they knew the rules of all the rivers around here, because some rivers were different, and even some parts of some rivers were different.

"No more bait," McCain said. "No more keeping fish. Understand?"

"No, yes, please," Ivanonov said. The other two men nodded their heads and looked at Jack.

McCain took the fish on their stringer and left the men with citations for a couple different violations. He wondered if they would pay the fines.

When he left the three Russians, he decided he'd drive on up the Yakima and check on the last few anglers on the river.

CHAPTER 10

Al Stephens rode comfortably up the trail above Rimrock Lake. He and seven other members of the Central Washington Backcountry Horsemen's club were heading up a couple days early for their annual 4th of July trip into the high Cascades. The group was packing in wall tents and enough food and gear to have a good four-day stay.

The string of horses and riders was about a third of the way up the trail to the Twin Sisters Lakes where they would camp when Stephens spotted a cluster of yellowish-white bones down the hill in some brush. The riders occasionally saw bones of dead animals on their outings into the mountains, so he didn't think much about it. That is until he looked a little closer and saw a large round bone that looked eerily like a human skull.

"Whoa," Stephens said to his horse as he gently pulled on the reins and pointed toward the bones. "Hey, what does that look like to you guys?"

One of the younger members, named Dave Davis, dismounted and walked the forty yards down the hill to get a closer look.

"Holy shit," Davis said. "It's a human skull. And there are more bones here too."

One of the other club members, Del Newman, was a volunteer sheriff's deputy, so he took over.

"We need to get word down to the sheriff's office right away," Newman said. "And we need to stay away from the skull and bones. Davis and I will ride back down to the corrals. You guys can continue up to set up camp. We'll come join you as soon as we can."

McCain was at Clear Lake, just up the road from the corrals, when he heard the call. Dispatch knew his location, and because he was the closest law enforcement officer in the area, they asked if he'd run over and talk to a couple horse riders who claimed to have found a human skull.

It took him only seven minutes to get down the hill to the corrals. As he pulled up, he saw a couple men standing next to horses tied to the top rail of a fence. He told Jack to stay and jumped out to chat with the men.

"Hey, Luke," the older man said. "Haven't seen you in a while."

McCain knew Newman because he had purchased his personal truck from him a year ago. Besides being a volunteer deputy, Newman was the sales manager at the local Toyota dealership.

"Hey, Del," McCain said. "So, what's going on here?"

Newman introduced McCain to Davis, and then the two horsemen told McCain the story of finding the skull and bones.

"How far up the trail is it?" McCain asked.

He'd been up the trail on foot a couple of times over the years, once to check on a potential elk hunter who was reported to have shot a branch-antlered bull elk without the appropriate tag. And he'd helped a couple of the WDFW hatchery guys pack some cutthroat trout fry up to three of the high mountain lakes on the trail.

"I'd say it's about two and a half miles in," said Davis.

McCain remembered the trail. Like many that led off the highway, it was a steep climb for the first mile or so and mostly uphill the rest of the way.

"Any chance there's another mount around here I could use to get up there?" McCain asked the men.

"I'm guessing they'd have a horse that you could use around here somewhere," Newman said. "Let's see if we can find Mr. Patterson."

The Pattersons ran the Indian Creek Corrals and rented horses to folks during the summer for horse-packing trips and day rides. In the fall they hired out to pack hunters into the backcountry. Twenty minutes later, Ray Patterson, proprietor of the outfit, had a horse saddled and ready to go for McCain.

"You might get another horse ready, Mr. Patterson," McCain said. "There's a sheriff's deputy on his way from Yakima right now, and he'll need to get up there too."

"Will do," Patterson said.

With that McCain hoisted himself up into the saddle, and then, after Patterson adjusted his stirrups, they started for the trailhead. Jack ran along with the riders, zigging and zagging through the woods, staying slightly ahead of the three horses.

McCain wasn't an experienced horse rider, but he knew the basics. And with the gentle mare Patterson had let him ride, he had no troubles guiding her up the mountain trail to where the skull and bones were located.

"It's right up here," Newman said. "Let's stop and walk from here."

They all dismounted, and McCain called Jack.

"Sit, Jack," he said to the dog. "Stay."

Jack obeyed. In fact, he lay down to take a breather from the run up the hill.

McCain walked a short way up the trail with Newman, and

when they reached the spot where they could see the bones, McCain told Newman to wait there while he walked down to get a closer look. There was no flesh left on any of the bones, but some were marked by yellowish-brown stains, which to McCain meant they hadn't been exposed to the elements all that long. It had been a sunny summer so far, and the sun can bleach bones in a matter of a few weeks.

He studied the area around the bones, which were scattered in a ten-foot circle. It was his guess that not all the bones were there, probably because coyotes or other animals had packed some off. There were fresh boot tracks, which he assumed were left by Davis, but he saw an older boot print too. It was so old it could have been left by a hunter last fall, but still he made a note of it. He also found strands of long black hair caught on a ceanothus bush farther down the hill.

"Damn," McCain said to himself as he swatted at a swarm of mosquitoes that had magically appeared.

He turned and headed back up the hill to the men and horses.

"I need to get back down to the corrals as quickly as possible," McCain declared as he smacked a mosquito on his neck. "I sure appreciate your help, but if you guys want to catch up with your group, you can go ahead."

The men climbed back on their mounts and headed up the hill while McCain and Jack headed back down the trail. McCain needed to reach Agent Sinclair as quickly as possible. When he returned to the corrals, he hustled over to his truck and radioed dispatch. He asked the dispatcher if she could patch him through to Agent Sinclair of the FBI.

"We could if we had her number," the dispatcher replied.

Like most people nowadays, McCain didn't know anyone's phone number. They were all programed into his phone, not in his head, so he had to check his phone contacts to find Sinclair's number. He found it and gave it to the dispatcher.

"Sending you through now," the dispatcher said.

McCain heard a phone ringing and then Sinclair's voice saying, "Hello, you've reached Agent Sinclair. I'm not available right now. If you leave a number, I'll get back to you as soon as I can."

"Hey, it's McCain," he said. "There's another body. Well, it's not a body, more like a bunch of bones. But I've found some long black hair nearby. I think we need to seriously consider that this is the work of the same killer. I'm guessing the sheriff will be calling in the FBI if he comes to the same conclusion. Just wanted to give you a heads up and thought you might want to get up here sooner rather than later. Call our dispatch to get directions up here."

McCain asked the dispatcher to give the coordinates and phone number of the Patterson's horse outfit to Sinclair if she called in and they couldn't raise him on the radio.

"Oh, and tell her to bring some mosquito spray if she comes," McCain told the dispatcher. "Those blood suckers up on the hill are as big as woodpeckers."

He then went over to the Patterson's place to let them know there might be a phone call from the FBI, and they might need another horse.

"We'll make sure you are paid for the horses," McCain said. "It's my guess you'll be renting a few more during the next couple of days. Thanks for all your help."

With that McCain turned, patted his hip, and Jack fell in place. They walked back to his truck to wait for the deputy to show or Sinclair to call. As he sat by the highway, in the gravel lot next to the horse corrals, an older 80s vintage Chevy pickup pulled up. McCain recognized the driver as Jim Kingsbury, a sixty-something man who always wore a Crocodile Dundee-style Australian hat, and any one of a plethora of t-shirts with humorous or political sayings on them.

Kingsbury was a local character in the Naches area, obviously retired because you'd see him at just about any time of day driving around or parked at one café or another. What he had retired from, McCain didn't know, but the guy had the gift of gab. There were times when McCain was glad to chat with the gentleman, and other times he would cringe when he saw him coming.

When McCain saw the Chevy pull up next to him in the parking lot, he figured a little talk with Kingsbury might be a good way to pass a few minutes while he awaited the others.

"Hey, Jim," McCain said. "What you doing up this way?"

McCain took note of the blue t-shirt that Kingsbury was wearing. In bold white print across the chest it read, IT'S BETTER TO WAKE UP AND PEE THAN PEE AND WAKE UP.

"I heard the silvers were biting at Rimrock," Kingsbury said. "That asshole Frank Dugdale told me so. He's a damn liar. You should never trust a guy with three first names."

McCain laughed. He knew that Kingsbury and Dugdale were good buddies and that Kingsbury was probably not terribly upset at his friend.

"Well, you tell him they're catching two-pound cutthroats up at Dumbbell," McCain said. "He'll hike in there and be lucky to catch a twelve-incher."

"That S.O.B wouldn't hike two hundred yards for a five-pounder," the older man said. "I'll get him back sometime. So, what's going on up here?"

"Some horse riders found some bones. Not sure what they are, but we're going to check them out."

"Connected to those bodies that were found up in these hills?" Kingsbury asked. "There's scuttlebutt around town there might be another Gary Ridgeway running around these parts."

Gary Ridgeway was infamously known as the Green River Killer, one of the most prolific serial killers in United States history. He preyed on teenage girls and young women during the 80s and 90s and dumped many of their bodies along the Green River in Western Washington. When he was finally caught, he was convicted of murdering 49 women, although he had confessed to killing seventy-one.

"Oh, I don't think that's what we are dealing with here," McCain said. "But the sheriff needs to take a look at it. I really am not involved in the investigation."

The two men talked for a while longer. McCain told Kingsbury to go give Clear Lake a try if he wanted to catch a mess of trout to eat. When he'd been up there a little earlier in the day the folks fishing along the banks were having some good luck. It didn't hurt that the WDFW hatchery crews had been to the lake a couple days before and dumped a few thousand rainbows in the lake.

"Aw, I don't like the taste of those hatchery fish," Kingsbury said. "But I have developed a hankerin' for some of those silvers for the smoker. That damn Dugdale, I'll get him back when he's least expecting it."

With that, Kingsbury jumped in his pickup and drove away. As he did McCain noticed a new bumper sticker on the back of the truck. It read: *I'm not a Gynecologist, but I'd be glad to take a look.* McCain just smiled and shook his head.

Williams was the deputy who showed up from the Yakima County Sheriff's Office. He pulled in next to McCain's truck, rolled down the window and said, "I'm getting tired of this."

McCain filled him in on what he had seen and asked Williams if he was ready to saddle up.

"Can I walk?" Williams asked. "Me and horses don't get along too good."

"You can if you like, but it's a pretty good haul. Over two miles uphill, almost the whole way."

"Aw, geeze. Okay, but get me the calmest old mare in the string. The last time I had to ride a four-legged creature into the hills, I got a nasty old mule that spent half the time swerving into low limbs trying to knock me off."

"I'll talk to Patterson," McCain said. "The mare I rode up on a bit ago was pretty easygoing. I had no problems with her. Maybe we should switch, and you should ride her."

And, that's what they did. After some stirrup adjusting, Williams was on the chestnut-colored mare McCain had ridden earlier, and McCain was astride a dapple-gray mare. They gave the horses a tap on the sides with the heels of their boots and they were off.

On the way up the trail, Jack again flanked them, running just off the trail as the two men talked.

"I thought maybe Stratford would get this call. Isn't he the guy patrolling the passes now?" McCain asked.

"We both work the passes and kind of trade off," Williams said. "He's off for a few days, so I'm the guy. After looking at the bones, any idea how long they've been out here?"

McCain described the coloration of the bones and gave his opinion on the question. In his investigations over the years of dead animals, many that had been poached, he had a good idea how long it took for bodies to decompose in the mountains. He wouldn't swear to it, nor would he have to, but his guess was the body had been up here about nine months, since maybe October.

The men were having no trouble moving up the trail until a small rattlesnake decided to cross right in front of Williams's horse. The mare's ears went back, her eyes got about three times larger than normal, and she gave one big snort before she started bucking like a rodeo bronc.

"HANG ON!" McCain yelled at Williams who upon further inspection didn't need the advice. He was hanging on for dear life.

"WHOA! WHOA!" Williams screamed at the mare while pulling back on the reins.

But the horse kept crow-hopping and snorting. Luckily, Williams was a big, strong guy, and even though the judges would have disqualified him for holding on with two hands, he otherwise might have made a decent score. He lasted the full eight seconds before he decided to bail off to one side.

Williams actually stuck the landing, hitting on both feet, standing perfectly straight as the horse spun away and ran back down the trail toward the corrals.

McCain was amazed at the whole event, and after he saw that Williams was okay, other than maybe needing some clean shorts, he started laughing.

"Dang, that was some ride," McCain said to Williams between laughing fits. "You sure you and horses don't get along?"

"Not funny," Williams said. "About the only thing I like less than horses are rattlesnakes. Where is that thing? I'm going to kill it."

"I don't think Mr. Patterson would appreciate that. I think old Buttercup there is one of his best ponies."

"Not the horse, the snake!" Williams exclaimed. "I coulda been killed."

McCain laughed again and looked around for Jack. The dog was sitting about twenty feet away with a happy dog look on his face. It seems he had enjoyed the rodeo performance immensely.

When they finally arrived at the bones, Williams took his time looking around and taking photos with his cell phone. Then he taped the area off with yellow tape that he'd carried with him in a small daypack. The crime scene folks would be back up to the site the next day for a more thorough look around, but Williams had enough information to give them a report when he returned to Yakima.

On the way back down the hill McCain offered to let Williams ride the gray horse, but Williams said there wasn't enough gold in Fort Knox to get him back on another horse. The whole walk down the trail Williams discussed his dislike for riding something that had a brain the size of a tennis ball, weighed ten times what he did, and could squash a man like a roach. McCain just chuckled as Jack searched around every tree and rock for another pesky squirrel to hassle.

When McCain and Williams returned to the corrals it was obvious the arrival of a rider-less horse had created a bit of a stir. Patterson was getting another horse ready to take up the trail himself, to make sure the men were okay.

Meanwhile, the ABC-TV van had shown up, and there stood Simon Erickson. It seems they had been monitoring their police scanner, as most news stations and print reporters were apt to do, and he had headed up the mountain to see if he could get enough to report on the story of the human bones found on the trail.

When Erickson saw Williams leading the way on foot, with McCain riding behind, he thought Williams had been caught by the horseman and was being transported to jail. His lucky day. He swung his camera around at the two men and began filming. Once he realized both men were law enforcement officers, he took a different tack.

"Would one of you officers have da time to give me a short interview?" Erickson asked.

"Don't look at me," McCain said. "Deputy Williams is in charge here."

Williams gave McCain the same look he had when he was looking for the snake.

CHAPTER 11

McCain replayed the wild horse ride in his mind and laughed as he drove down the mountain. It had been a long day, and he was anxious to get home and get to bed. He was almost to Naches when his phone rang.

"Hey, I assume you got my message?" he said as he answered.

"What do you think?" Sinclair asked.

"It's him," McCain said. "Even though there was no way for me to tell if it was a woman or man by looking at the bones, seeing the long black hair nearby tells me it had to be a woman."

"How long dead?" she asked.

"I'd say nine months," McCain answered. "But that's just a guess. I know it's too late today, but it would be worth checking the reports for a woman gone missing around that time."

"I already did," she said. "After I got your message, I started checking immediately for anyone missing in the last twelve months that fits our other women's description."

"And?" McCain asked.

"Nothing," she said. "Or at least not yet. Of course, we have a few Native women who are still missing, but none from that timeframe."

"Has YSO officially asked for your help yet?"

"No, but I've notified my boss to let him know it is probably coming."

"I've got department meetings in the morning, so I won't be on the mountain tomorrow," McCain said. "I'm guessing Williams will be escorting you and the other investigators up to the bones. That is if you can get him on a horse again."

McCain told her what had transpired on the horse ride up the hill, and as he did, he started laughing and because he was laughing so did she.

"I wish I could have seen it," she said.

"Well, don't razz him about it too much," McCain said. "He's a little sensitive. "

McCain told her good luck and goodbye and then pushed the hang-up button on his steering wheel. He was starving, so as he got into Naches he decided to pull into the café to grab a quick bite. He parked, jumped out of the truck, and was headed to the front door of the restaurant when he looked down the sidewalk and saw a young man in a cowboy hat walking with a woman with long black hair. He took another look back as the guy took off his hat and walked to the driver's door of an older silver Honda. The woman got in the passenger's side, and off they went.

"Silver Honda," McCain said to himself. "Crap."

He ran down the sidewalk, but the little car was just rounding the corner. He was just fast enough to catch the first three letters of the license plate.

McCain ran back to his truck and took off after the car. There were two ways out of town from where he was, and he took a guess at which way the car went. He figured the guy was heading to the highway and turned and headed that way. But when he got there, he saw no silver Hondas.

Doubling back, he headed to the old highway, and turned east. He drove slowly and looked up a couple side roads.

Nothing. By now the car could be headed about six different directions, down the highway to Yakima, or up the highway to the mountains. At least he had the partial on the license plate. That was going to have to do for now. He wrote the letters down on a little notepad he kept in his shirt pocket and turned to go back to the café.

He thought more about it and realized that with who-knows-how-many silver Hondas still on the road from the 1990s and with about 5,000 younger women with long black hair in the area, the chances that those two things together meant anything at all was a longshot.

At the table, after he had ordered up a burger and fries, he started thinking about the Honda he had seen coming down into the Wenas that day back in April. The car and the guy were definitely out of place, and the timing was about right for when the body of the Alverez woman would have been dumped.

He was pissed at himself for not getting the license plate on the rig at the time, but it was what it was. He'd have Sinclair or Williams run the plates to see if they could connect the first three letters he'd gotten earlier with a 1990s silver Honda.

Seeing the cowboy with the girl a few minutes earlier made him wonder about other aspects. Did the killer know these women? Or did he abduct them in some kind of Ted Bundy way, getting them to assist him to his car and then knock them on the head and throw them in the trunk?

He had looked at the skull on the mountain pretty closely today, and he hadn't seen any cracks in the bone. Nor had the coroner found any kind of damage to the heads of the other two women found in the mountains.

So far the sheriff's investigators hadn't found any link at all between the two women found earlier. Their paths didn't seem to cross anywhere. They lived in two different areas of the valley, and there seemed to be no overlap socially. The Green River

Killer had preyed on prostitutes and drug addicts, but the first two women seemed to lead normal lives with normal jobs.

He also started thinking about the killer. The guy had to be in some kind of shape if he had carried the woman, if it was a woman, up the Twin Sisters trail. McCain had packed a fifty-pound pack of water and fish up that trail, and it had been a chore. The same was true of the other two body sites. A person, probably a man, had to be in pretty good shape to pack someone that far from the road.

Or maybe the killer had used a horse or mule. He made another note in his book to have Sinclair check with the Pattersons to get the names of any people who might have rented a horse for one day, or overnight, during October or November. That was prime time for big game hunting along the eastern slopes of the Cascades, so his guess was there was a pretty long list of people who had rented horses.

She should check with any of the other outfitters too, to see if someone had rented a horse for one or two days during that period. They had the disappearance dates of the other two women. They should cross reference those dates, too, with any of the area horse packing operations.

As McCain was thinking about everything, something else was nagging at him. It was another idea to check out, but he couldn't quite put his finger on it. About that time his burger and fries came, and as an afterthought, he asked the waitress to put the meal in a to-go box. He just wanted to get home, so he grabbed the box, jumped in the truck and headed down the highway toward home.

The next morning was full of meetings, the one part of the job McCain could definitely do without. His boss was a great guy, but he loved to hear himself talk, as did a couple of the other folks in the Region 3 office. Meetings that should take about ten minutes would drag on endlessly.

As one of the biologists droned on about something, McCain wondered how Sinclair was doing with Williams up on the mountain. Was she an experienced rider? And, although he thought he knew the answer to the question, he wondered if Williams had tried riding another horse up the trail. He replayed the whole bucking bronc show from the day before and started to chuckle. It was about then he heard his name.

"McCain? McCain?" the woman's voice asked. "Did you hear my question?"

Damn, McCain thought. It was Andrea Parker, the head fish biologist for Region 3. She and McCain had a little history. About a year after he'd moved back to Yakima, she had taken a shining to him, and they had dated a few times. She was a pretty woman, very smart and very nice, but there just never were any sparks. At least there weren't any for him. Evidently, she had felt a little differently, and when he told Parker that he didn't think the relationship was worth pursuing, she didn't take it too well. He wanted to scream, "Get over it" at her so many times. It had been almost eight years for crying out loud! But he had always just smiled when she tried to get under his skin.

"I did hear your question, Andrea," McCain said. "But once again you are asking the wrong person."

If he remembered correctly, she was talking about bull trout in the Little Naches River before he had zoned out. In these meetings she almost always was.

The bull trout was now listed as a threatened species under the U.S. Endangered Species Act, and one of the jobs the WDFW police officers were being pushed to do was to keep a close eye on anglers fishing in waters where the bull trout lived and spawned.

The average angler barely knew a walleye from a bass, so to them a trout was a trout. If they caught a bull trout, about 90% of them would bonk the thing on the head and cook it over the fire in a skillet with fried potatoes and onions. He'd told Andrea that one time, and she got this horrible look on her face, like she'd just been told someone was killing starving children in India. If she and the other fish biologists had their say on what the enforcement officers did, they would be watching the rivers for bull trout poachers 24-7.

When McCain was a kid, everyone called bull trout "dolly varden," and you could go up to some holes on the Tieton and Naches Rivers and catch a whole creel full of the things. The biologists back in the day thought of them as scrap fish. Bull trout are veracious feeders, and all you had to do was run a Mepps or Rooster Tail spinner in front of them and it was fish on. They were big fish too. The state record bull trout was caught out of the Tieton River, right below Rimrock Dam back in 1961. The fish weighed twenty-two pounds, eight ounces.

Of course, that was way before the biologists determined that bull trout numbers were threatened. Some people, including Andrea Parker, had spent their entire careers on one small watershed, working to bring the bull trout population back up to acceptable numbers.

McCain thought it was admirable of her to be so passionate about one fish species, but if you talked to the average person around the area, they really couldn't care less. But someone had to do it, McCain knew, and she was the perfect woman for the job.

"You need to talk to Hargraves about that," McCain said, throwing poor old Stan directly under the bus.

If looks could kill, McCain would be dead, because Hargraves was staring daggers at him.

When the meetings finally ended, primarily because it was lunch time, and most of the workers there required "a duty-free lunch hour," McCain went over to Hargraves and told him he owed him one.

"You're damn right you do," Hargraves said and left it at that.

CHAPTER 12

He was finally headed back out into the field at two o'clock. He jumped in his truck, turned on the engine and checked the outside thermometer. It showed ninety-six degrees. During some Julys and Augusts in Central Washington, the high temperatures would top ninety degrees every day for weeks on end. On the hot days, when McCain kept the dog at home, Jack lounged around inside the house because it was air conditioned. McCain figured it would do the dog good to get outside, so he swung in and picked him up on the way up Highway 12 to do some checks on anglers on the river and a few of the lakes.

It was the third of July, and the campgrounds along the rivers were filled with people from all over the state. Travel trailers were parked next to tent trailers parked next to motor homes. And in between there were tents of all colors and sizes. Many campers just liked being out of town, hanging around a campfire, enjoying a hot dog cooked over the fire and a cold beer.

Some liked to fish on their camping outings, although many would opt to do so without purchasing a fishing license. Why spend the money on a license if it was only going to be used once or twice? So it was a busy time for McCain, checking to see if everyone was fishing legally. And heaven forbid if someone had caught and killed a bull trout. Andrea Parker would want them hung up by their thumbs.

As he was driving through Naches he looked over at the café and saw Jim Kingsbury's truck parked out front. McCain slowed and turned in. He wanted to ask the man a couple questions.

He parked, left the truck running with the AC on so Jack could keep cool, locked the doors with his key fob, and walked into the café. Kingsbury was sitting with another man who McCain recognized as Frank Dugdale, the man Kingsbury had been cussing the day before.

As he walked up to the two men sitting at the counter, he stirred the pot a little, "I heard the silvers turned on up at Rimrock."

"Bullshit," said Kingsbury. The man was attired in cargo shorts, flip-flops and a red t-shirt that said in bold white letters: BAN SHREDDED CHEESE—MAKE AMERICA GRATE AGAIN. His Crocodile Dundee hat was sitting on the counter.

Dugdale just grinned.

"Hey, I got a couple of questions for you two," McCain said as he grabbed a seat at the counter next to Kingsbury. "You guys know most of the people around here. You know a younger guy, stands about six feet or a bit more, wears a cowboy hat and drives an older silver Honda? Might have a girlfriend with long black hair."

"I've seen them," said Dugdale. "The girl is a looker, for sure."

"Yeah, I've seen them too," said Kingsbury. "But I don't know either of them. They've been hanging around town for the past couple weeks. Might be here to work in the orchards."

It was cherry season in the Yakima Valley. Growers from the Tri-Cities up to Wenatchee and beyond grow and ship cherries, and when the fruit is ready to pick, in June and July, thousands of pickers are needed. Many of the pickers migrate with the work, starting in early June down near Pasco where the fruit ripens first, and follow the jobs up the valley as the cherries in the higher elevations are ready to pick.

"You know anyone else around who drives a 90s era silver Honda?" McCain asked.

"Those damned foreign cars all look alike to me," Kingsbury said.

"Not just the foreign cars," Dugdale said. "Fords look like Toyotas, and Mercedes look like Chevys. The SUVs all look alike. You can't tell one from the other. What happened to the days when car designers wanted their cars to look different than everyone else's?"

The man with three first names was right, of course. McCain had often thought the same thing and wondered why someone would spend $80,000 on a SUV made by BMW when they could get one from Ford that looked almost the same for half the price.

"So, you don't know anyone around here with a silver Honda, 1990s vintage?" McCain repeated his question.

Both men sat and contemplated the question a bit more. They both shook their heads.

"Not that I can think of," Kingsbury said. "But if we see one, should we call you?"

"No, not necessary," McCain said. "There'll probably be about a hundred of them coming through town over the next few days."

Highway 12 and Highway 410 were both used heavily during the summer to get from the west side of the state to the east side. Many people from the Puget Sound area drove to Yakima and other cities in Eastern Washington to get away from the masses, and to enjoy some sun and fun. Instead of traveling on the busy I-90 freeway, they would opt for the more leisurely, picturesque drive over one of the other east/west passes. They came to play in the water, or golf, or take wine tours. And they came to fish.

"But if you see any other shady-looking characters that resemble Frank here, give me a holler," McCain added.

He thanked the men and headed back out to the cool of the air-conditioned truck cab.

As he was heading up Highway 12 near the "Y" where 410 and 12 merged, he saw the oversized black sedan of Agent Sinclair heading his way. He flashed his lights at her and pulled off the highway on a gravel turn out, but she blew right past him.

"Well, that's a fine how-do-you-do," McCain said to Jack.

A second later his cellphone was ringing.

McCain pushed the Bluetooth button on his steering wheel and said, "I didn't think you saw me."

"I saw you, but I need to get back to the office," Sinclair said. "As of ten minutes ago, the FBI is officially on the case. I found the black hair you said you saw, and by the size of leg bones, the crime scene people believe it is another woman. So, after Williams talked to the sheriff, they have asked us to come in and take the lead."

"Kinda saw that coming," McCain said.

"I'd really like to talk to you," she said. "But I have to go file about six reports to get the ball rolling. Can we meet for dinner later?"

"Sure," McCain said. "Let's meet at that Japanese steakhouse out by the airport. You know the one?"

"Yeah, a group of us met there for lunch a couple weeks ago. See you there about seven."

And she was gone.

McCain finished his day up along the Tieton River, checking anglers on the river and at a couple small gravel pits that sat next to the highway. His mode of operation was to pull in and just watch people for a bit. He studied them and their reaction to his arrival. The nervous ones, who might not have licenses, or had a fish or two over their limit, would always make a move. And McCain would nab them. When they didn't see his truck, he would keep an eye on them and watch what they did. Then, when he contacted them in person, he would ask them questions to which he already knew the answer.

One group of three younger guys he watched for a bit had caught three trout in rapid succession: bang, bang, bang. That told McCain they had it figured out and probably had several more trout in the cooler, where they'd put the three he had seen them catch.

McCain, with Jack at his side, walked up behind the group a couple minutes later and asked, "How's fishing, boys?"

They turned, saw he was a wearing a badge, and started hem-hawing.

"We've got a couple, but it's been pretty slow," the biggest of the three guys said.

"A couple, huh? Are you keeping any?"

"Naw," the bigger guy said, obviously the spokesman for the group.

"Can I see your fishing licenses and IDs?" McCain asked. "Whatcha got in the cooler?"

"Just some beer," the spokesman said as he handed McCain his license and ID.

He checked the other two licenses and said, "You know, you guys can keep five trout apiece in this lake."

"Yeah, we know," the shortest guy said.

"No fish then on a stringer or in a cooler?" McCain asked again.

"No, sir," the short one answered. All of sudden he was the talker.

Jack moved over and started sniffing the cooler. The big guy was trying to shoo him away.

"Okay, I'm going to be straight up with you fellas," McCain explained. "I was watching you from my truck over there, and in five minutes I saw you land three trout and toss them in the cooler. So I know you have kept some. The only reason you might lie to me about that is maybe you have a few more than three in there."

When it was all said and done, McCain counted twenty-two trout in the ice chest. He wrote each of the men a citation for catching over their limit and told them not to do it again. That, he knew, was like telling a post to stop standing there looking stupid.

He talked to a few other anglers around the lake and checked their licenses. A middle-aged man in a floppy hat and a Hawaiian shirt like Tom Selleck used to wear on the TV show *Magnum PI* said he was glad that McCain caught the guys with too many fish.

"They were loud and foul-mouthed and every time they caught a fish they would hoot and holler," that man said. "It got old fast. I was just about to go over there and have a few words with them when you showed up. I hope you gave them a big, fat ticket."

McCain told the floppy hat man that getting into it with guys like that probably wasn't the best idea, and if he was to have problems again, to give him a call. Then he gave the man his card and continued on.

He went and checked several anglers on the river, and luckily, none had any bull trout in their possession. He would put that in his daily report so that Andrea Parker would know he was doing his job.

The steakhouse out by the airport was one of those where a bunch of strangers sat around a giant sizzling hot grill, and the chef would come out in a tall white hat and cook your meal in front of you. It was like Benihana, but since Yakima was too small to actually have a Benihana, this was the next best thing. The restaurant also had several booths in a separate area where diners could forgo the show and just have a nice quiet meal. When Sinclair arrived, that is what they decided to do.

"So how was your day?" she asked after they had been seated.

"Oh, you know," he said. "I sat through about four hours of mind-numbingly boring discussion about streamside habitat and the effect it has on spawning bull trout. Then Jack and I went out and harassed some trout fishermen."

"Wow," she said. "Why didn't I become a game warden?"

"That's fish and wildlife police officer," he corrected. "Yeah, you don't know what kind of fun you're missing out on. And how about you? Did you enjoy your little horse ride up into the Cascades?"

Sinclair said she actually did like the ride up the trail to the bones. When she was a teenager her friend had horses, and they rode them often. She always enjoyed riding, even if it was on business.

McCain had never quite understood the relationship that some females had with horses. It was like a mystical bond.

"Did Williams ride up the hill?" he asked.

"Nope, he walked," she said.

"How'd they get the bones down?"

"The coroner placed them in a body bag and then strapped the bag onto a pack horse."

"Anyone find anything else around the bones of interest, besides the hair?"

"No, not really."

"Did you see the old boot track?" he asked.

"No, I missed that," she said. "Where was it?"

"About five yards north of the hair. It was only a partial, and fairly old. Coulda been from a hunter or who knows. I took a few photos on my phone. Laid my flashlight next to it for size comparison. I saw you FBI guys do that on TV once."

"Wow, writing tickets to poor fishermen just trying to catch enough trout for dinner AND an investigator. Look at you."

"Aw, shucks," McCain said.

"I'll need you to send me those photos by the way," she said.

They chatted about the site, and the bones, and the other bodies through the rest of dinner. McCain finally remembered to tell her about the guy in the silver Honda coming out of the mountains on the same road where the second body had been dumped. He also told her about the silver Honda in Naches, with the cowboy and the girl with the long black hair. He gave her the partial license plate from his notepad and saw the reminder he'd made about the horse rental places.

"I was thinking about how someone might get a body up that trail by himself," McCain elaborated. "First off, if he packed the body on his back or shoulders, he's gotta be in fantastic shape. Then I thought he might have gotten up there the way you did today, or I did yesterday, by horseback. So, it might be worth checking with the Indian Spring Corrals folks, and any other place that rents horses for day trips to riders and hunters, and get the names of anyone who had rented a horse in October or November last year, and March and April this year."

"Good idea," she said.

"It's probably nothing but might be worth checking out."

"You never know when something is going to help," Sinclair said. "When we finally sent out the language in the letters from the Unabomber, it was the guy's brother who helped identify him."

"You mean that John Krasinski guy?" McCain asked, knowing that he'd given her the wrong name.

"Kaczynski," she corrected him. "John Krasinski is the guy who played Jim on *The Office*. Good thing you only have to run down poachers who escape from jail."

McCain started laughing and told her he'd given her the wrong name to see if she'd catch it.

"Riiight," she said.

As they were walking out to their vehicles after dinner, McCain said, "I know I'm not officially part of this investigation, but I've been giving it a lot of thought, and I'd like to help where I can."

Sinclair thanked McCain, jumped in the black beast, and roared off into the night.

Before McCain turned his truck out of the parking lot he typed her a text: *Why do Oregon Ducks eat cereal from the box? Because they choke whenever they get near a bowl.*

When he awoke the next morning, there was a text waiting for him on his phone. It read: *Do you know what WSU grads say to Oregon grads? You want fries with that?*

Touché, McCain thought to himself.

CHAPTER 13

The 4th of July was going to be a hot one. Close to 100 degrees according to the Storm Chaser weather dude on the local NBC station. McCain always wondered why the big wigs at the TV station would promote their weather forecasters as storm chasers. This wasn't Kansas or someplace with tornados tearing up trailer parks now and again. Nor was it the southeast where they were hit by a hurricane about every other week. This was Central Washington. This area had two storms a year, and those were winter storms in December or January. He figured the other ten months of the year the storm chasers were sitting on their thumbs because, besides a rain shower once in a rare while, your average third grader could look outside and tell you what the weather was. But the storm chaser name sounded good, and McCain guessed the aging viewers of the local news at six didn't really give a crap.

He also had to laugh at the weather person at the CBS affiliate. Her name was Wendy Storm. Not Windy, but Wendy, although when she said her name it came out as Windy. Of course, the local viewers believed it to be a made-up name, but she had taken to Facebook and Instagram to assure the viewers that no, really, that was her given name.

McCain thought to get people to believe her, she should end each one of her weather forecasts by saying, "And that's the weather, I'm Wendy Storm. I shit you not."

All three of the weather broadcasters at the local TV stations basically said the same thing about the 4th of July. It was going to be hotter than the hubs of hell.

While most people had the day off to celebrate our country's independence, WDFW police officers were on the clock. Many of the celebrations started early in the campgrounds and other gathering areas, and usually by the time it was dark enough for fireworks, some of the partiers were already lit. It always led to some crazy stuff.

Drunken people and illegal fireworks were always a bad combination, and McCain had spent several 4th of Julys helping to fight small brush fires, trying to keep the county from burning up. Over the years there had been a couple of squabbles that he'd had to deal with as well. Beer and hot weather had a tendency to exacerbate any conflicts amongst revelers.

The fires, of course, were all calls that the district fire departments were supposed to handle. And the fights were something the Yakima County Sheriff's Office should be dealing with, but again, Yakima County was a big one, and anyone with a badge was put to work dealing with the issues of the holiday. So, it was no surprise when McCain heard the dispatcher call for assistance at a campground up Highway 12, not far from where he'd checked the anglers at the small lake the day before.

According to dispatch, there was a fight brewing in the campground. The lady who called in to report the altercation said she thought one of the people had a gun. McCain heard Deputy Stratford, who was patrolling the passes, respond and say he was probably thirty minutes away.

"Crap," he said to Jack who was riding in the seat next to him. "I guess we had better go check it out."

He jumped on the radio and told dispatch he was ten minutes away and would go have a look.

When he pulled into the campground, he saw a group of about fifteen people all in a big circle. Usually when a police rig pulls into an area where something is happening, people in the group tend to scatter. And some of them did when they saw McCain's rig with the lights in the grill flashing red and blue, and the big badge emblem on the door. But not all of them did.

McCain opened the door, jumped out and called Jack. He scanned the group of mostly men and wasn't surprised to see the big guy from the lake yesterday right in the middle of things. The little guy from the lake was next to him, and they seemed to be the focus of attention of several other men, and one really pissed-off woman.

"Okay," McCain said in a loud voice. "What's going on here?"

It helped that he was about three inches taller than anyone in the group, including the big guy, and with the hot weather, he was wearing his short sleeve duty shirt. One time when McCain was helping with a hunter's safety class filled with twelve-year-olds, one of the kids in the class took a good long look at him and said, "Wow dude, you're ripped." McCain was hoping the people in this bunch were thinking the same thing. It always made things easier if they did.

"These two assholes started making lewd remarks to my wife," said a man in a green tank top with a bandana tied around his head.

"Yeah," the mad woman said. She was wearing a matching green tank top, her auburn hair tied up in a bun.

"Okay, here is what we are going to do," McCain said. "You two," he pointed to the two trout fishermen from the pond the day before, "are going to go over and stand by my truck."

"And you two," he pointed to the man and woman in the matching tank tops, "are going to go over there and stand by the outhouse."

At that the woman made a puking noise and said, "Really? That thing stinks like shit. Even the flies won't go near it."

"Go," he said and pointed. To the mob he said, "And the rest of you go on back to your campsites. Now, whoever called this in said someone had a gun. If I even think I see a gun, I am going to arrest the whole campground, and you'll all be in lockup in Yakima until Labor Day. So don't push it."

He took a look around and saw an older gentleman sitting in a lawn chair, watching the lively discussion while he enjoyed a beer next to a tent trailer. McCain walked over to him.

"I'm guessing you're a neutral party in whatever this is," McCain said to the man. "Can you tell me what happened?"

The man told McCain he hadn't heard the two guys who were standing by his truck say anything, but they might have laughed or made a face or something when the woman had walked by. He said he thought the gal in the green shirt had maybe had one too many beers and was kind of parading around like Miss America. He guessed she didn't like the way those guys looked at her or laughed or whatever.

"She disappeared," he explained. "And all of sudden here comes her biker-wannabe-husband, looking for a fight."

"Okay, thanks," McCain said to the man. "Appreciate it."

He then went over to the two trout fishermen, who basically told the same story, leaving out the part about maybe laughing at the gal.

"She's just drunk," the shorter guy said.

"Okay, where is your camp?" McCain asked.

The two men pointed to a big green Cabela's tent pitched under a tall pine tree close to the river.

"Stay here a minute longer," McCain said. He walked over to the couple in the matching tank tops and said to the woman, "Tell me what happened."

"Those bastards started insulting my wife," the man in the bandana said.

"I didn't ask you what happened," McCain said to the man. "I asked your wife."

"I wassh getting bored and show I deshided to go for a walk," she said slurring some of her words. "And thosh two assholes called me a prositu . . . a prosute . . . a whore."

"Where's your camp?" he asked the husband.

He pointed to the other end of the campground, about four hundred yards away, and said, "The white and blue trailer."

McCain told them to go back to their trailer and, talking directly to the lady, told them to take a little nap so they'd be wide awake when the fireworks started. He told them to stay at their end of the campground. And he gave them a stern warning that if he had to come back here again, people WERE going to go to jail, and that the sheriffs would get it all sorted out after the three-day weekend. He told them he was going to tell the two gentlemen over there the same thing.

"Gentlemen, my ash," the woman said under her beer-tainted breath.

"If you really want to spend your holiday in jail, just try me," McCain said.

He went and gave the two trout fishermen the same speech. They assured him they hadn't done or said a thing and promised to stay away from the drunken lady and her "mouth-breathing husband."

As McCain was walking back toward his truck a slight breeze blew by and he about gagged. The woman was right about one thing: the outhouse definitely stunk like shit. He looked around for Jack who had conveniently disappeared during McCain's speech to the campers and found him sitting right smack dab in front of a fat man sitting backwards on a picnic table bench. Jack was staring up longingly as the oversized man ate a foot-long hotdog, all slathered in mustard. McCain whistled for the dog, and Jack came on the run.

"I think you were wishful thinking there, bud," McCain said to Jack. "Come on, it's too damned hot out here to be dealing with all of this."

McCain followed Jack into the truck, fired it up and turned the AC on high. As they waited for the fan to blow cold McCain looked in the rearview mirror and saw an older silver Honda pass by on the highway. The car had gone by so quickly McCain hadn't gotten a good look at the driver, but he decided it was worth checking out. He jumped out ahead of a couple other rigs coming up the highway and kicked the Ford in the butt.

He didn't want to push the car, just get close enough to see who was driving. When he could read the license plate, he saw it had the same three first letters of the car he'd seen in Naches. He ran the plates on his computer and the registration showed the car was owned by a Chad Burke, age twenty-nine, with a last known address in North Bend, Washington.

As they neared the unincorporated enclave of Rimrock Retreat, the Honda slowed, the left turn signal came on, and the car turned into the Trout Lodge café. McCain followed and pulled in right next to the car.

McCain left the truck running for Jack and climbed out at the same time the driver of the Honda. The man was a couple inches shorter than McCain, and was, as the twelve-year-old kid in the hunter's ed class would say, ripped.

"It's a hot one, huh?" McCain said to the guy.

"Sure is," the man said. "And the AC in this old Honda here is struggling."

The two men walked through the door into the lobby where there was a soda fountain and a small freezer with tubs of ice cream inside.

"I was ready for something cool to drink," McCain said.

"They have the best ice cream cones here," the guy said. "You should try one."

"You must live around here," McCain said.

"No. Well, I guess I do now," the man said. "I came up from Colorado. I've been here for about ten months. I work for the river rafting company that runs trips down the Tieton River in September. Then I give ski lessons up at White Pass during the winter, and in the spring and summer I guide fly fishermen over on the Yakima River."

"Wow, each one of those is my dream job," McCain said. "You ever fish the Naches?"

"A couple times, but I'm so busy with clients on the Yakima, it's hard to get to other streams."

"There's some nice fish in the Naches, and people rarely fish it. I live close so I fish there quite a bit."

The gal at the counter finished scooping up two double-scoop ice cream cones and handed them to the men. The cowboy got a chocolate chip mint, and McCain went for a rocky road.

"I'm probably going to regret this," he said to Burke. "I'll be wearing half of it before I'm done."

The cowboy paid for his cone, said "good talking to ya, see ya around," and was heading for the door when McCain asked him, "Hey, didn't I see you with a pretty, dark-haired gal in Naches the other night?"

The man stopped, turned around, gave McCain a quizzical look and said, "Yeah, wow, you're pretty perceptive. I was on a date. Didn't go too well either." He smiled and walked out the door, jumped in his Honda and headed on up the highway.

McCain grabbed about twenty napkins and sat down to

eat his ice cream. As he licked away he thought about the little interaction he'd just had. Burke, the rafter/skier/fishing guide had been around when the three women had disappeared, and he was definitely strong enough to pack a dead body pretty much anywhere he wanted.

Burke hadn't lied to him when McCain had asked about being with a dark-haired woman, but according to Jim Kingsbury and Frank Dugdale, they'd seen the cowboy in the Honda with her at least one other time before. On the other hand, the cowboy hadn't said it was a first date, or his only date with the woman.

Something to ponder, McCain thought to himself. Then, with about one big dog bite left of his cone, he headed to the truck, opened the cab door, and gave the treat to Jack.

Driving back down Highway 12, McCain slowed at the campground where the ruckus had been earlier and looked it over carefully. Everyone seemed to be getting along. He thought about the husband and wife who were dressed in the same green tank tops and wondered what that was all about. He'd seen it other times on occasion and could never quite understand the appeal of dressing in the same shirt or same windbreaker as the wife.

He thought about his past relationships and wondered which one of his girlfriends would have been one of those women who wanted her man to wear matching sweatshirts. The only one he could think of was Andrea Parker.

"We dodged a bullet there," McCain said to his yellow dog and rubbed his ears. The dog licked his shirt where a glob of chocolate ice cream had landed.

The next day was a day off for McCain, and when it finally cooled down he threw on some cut-off jeans and some old sneakers, grabbed his trout rod and box of spinners and headed for the river with Jack. He loved fishing the river this time of year. It didn't get dark until 9:30, which gave him plenty of time in the coolness of the evening to wade from hole to hole looking for trout. Jack loved it too. The big yellow Lab was definitely a water dog, and if McCain didn't watch him, Jack would be splashing around right in the hole he was trying to fish.

Being on the river also gave him some solitude to think. The driver's license photo proved that Chad Burke was indeed the man's name, but McCain couldn't be sure that he was the driver of the silver Honda he'd seen in the spring coming down into the Wenas. The turkey hunter had said the guy he saw driving by in the Honda had on a cowboy hat, but McCain didn't remember seeing the driver in one. Burke kind of looked like the driver McCain remembered, but kind of didn't either. He just didn't know.

He was thinking again about Burke's coy answer to his question about being with a pretty woman with dark hair when a sixteen-inch rainbow trout nearly jerked his little ultra-light rod out of his hands. He forgot about everything for a few moments while he fought the fish.

CHAPTER 14

Two days later McCain was again patrolling up at White Pass. He had heard from reliable sources that the silvers were biting at Rimrock Lake, and he decided he should go up and make sure the anglers there were sticking to the regulations.

Most of the anglers trolled from boats to catch the little landlocked sockeye salmon, but a few fished off the rocks on the south side of the lake with pencil bobbers and whitefish flies tipped with maggots or white shoepeg corn.

Rimrock was a decent-sized lake, six miles long and a mile wide, but the little salmon were quite prolific there, which meant the thousands and thousands of fish competed for a limited food supply. Because there were too many fish and not enough food, the kokanee never got very big. A whopper at Rimrock was twelve-inches long, and most years the bigger fish were nine or ten inches in length.

Based on the overpopulation situation most every year, the state allowed anglers at Rimrock to keep 16 kokanee—called silvers by the locals—a day. And they were allowed to chum for the fish. Chumming was used to attract the feeding fish, and a good chum recipe consisted of eggshells, bran, powdered milk, and some salmon egg nectar. Every few minutes, an angler, either from the bank, or an anchored boat, would send a couple heaping scoops of chum into the water. It worked surprisingly well.

McCain took the Tieton Reservoir Road off Highway 12 at the east end of the lake and stayed on it as it followed the southern shoreline of the big reservoir. He saw several rigs parked up ahead in the gravel shoulder and wasn't surprised to see Jim Kingsbury's truck among the few other pickups and SUVs. He was guessing that Dugdale was with him down near the shoreline, fishing off the giant boulders that bordered the lake.

McCain parked his truck and got out to watch the anglers for a bit. Most were paying no attention to him, but two men saw him coming and started getting a little fidgety. McCain was climbing down the rocks to get to the group of anglers when he saw Kingsbury set the hook and fight a small, silvery fish to the bank.

When he turned around to put his fish in an ice chest, he saw McCain and said, "Cool it everyone, it's the law!"

"Looks like you're going to be able to satisfy that hankerin' for smoked silvers," McCain said as he kept an eye on the two jittery guys a ways down the bank. Suddenly they seemed like they needed to be somewhere, anywhere else. McCain walked right on by Kingsbury who was trying to tell him about the fish he had caught and made it down the bank seventy-five yards to where the two men were hustling out of there.

"Excuse me, guys," McCain said to the two. "Can we chat for a second?"

The two men stopped, and McCain caught up to them.

"Can I see your driver's licenses and fishing licenses? And before you start with some story about how your wife washed your fishing license with the laundry or you left it in your other pants, I can look on the computer in my truck and know within about thirty seconds if you purchased one or not. I'm feeling benevolent today, so don't lie to me, and I'll give you a warning."

Both guys couldn't get their driver's licenses out fast enough, apologizing immediately. McCain wrote their names down and told them he would share them with the other WDFW police officers in the area, and if they got caught again without a license their fine would be doubled.

As McCain returned, Dugdale asked, "Are you going to ask me if I have my license?"

"No, because I already checked on you and Jim," McCain said. He looked over at Kingsbury who was wearing a white t-shirt with DON'T TASE ME BRO! written in bold black letters on the front. "So I found the guy in the silver Honda. Have you guys seen him or the gal with the black hair around town again?"

"Yeah, I saw the guy once more," Dugdale said. "I was going to call you, but you said not to. He was at the hardware store in Naches. I didn't see what he was buying. I was in there to get some replacement pieces to one of my toilets and—"

"He doesn't care what you were buying," Kingsbury interrupted. "And to answer your question, no, I haven't seen him or that cute gal again. Too bad too, she was a looker. By the way, that was pretty nice of you to let those guys off with a warning."

"Yeah, well don't tell anyone," McCain said. "I might get a bad reputation."

About that time Dugdale set the hook on a fish and brought it quickly to shore. He took it off the hook and tossed it into the same cooler that Kingsbury was using.

"We're two short of our limits," Dugdale said as he shoveled another heaping scoop of chum out of a five-gallon bucket and tossed it into the lake near where their bobbers were standing erect on the water's surface.

After a quick thanks and a goodbye, McCain was back to his truck to finish his tour around the lake. He checked a few other bank anglers and stopped and checked a couple guys at the boat ramp on the north side of the lake to see how they had done. They too had caught their limits.

As he was driving back down the mountain toward Yakima he thought more about Chad Burke. McCain wondered what his shoe size was, and that reminded him he hadn't heard from Sinclair on what she had found out from the photos of the boot print he took up at the bones. And he thought about the woman with the long black hair he had seen only so briefly on the sidewalk in Naches that night. He wondered where she was right now.

The next morning, as McCain was getting ready for work and watching the morning news for the weather forecast, his phone started ringing. It was Sinclair.

"We have the identity of the woman found on the trail," she said. "Her name was Tandy Miller, and she was from Enumclaw. They ID'd her with dental records."

"Okay, that's different," McCain said. "She's not from the valley."

"No, but she had long black hair and was dumped on our side of the Cascades," Sinclair said. "Enumclaw is just over the hill, so definitely could be the same guy."

"Yeah," McCain said. "But why not dump the body on the west side of the mountains, or at least on the Highway 410 side? Enumclaw is a lot closer to this side via Chinook Pass."

Sinclair went on to tell him that after they'd searched in Central Washington for missing women fitting the description of the two women found earlier, they expanded the search to statewide and Miller's name had popped up.

"Sure enough, the dentals matched," Sinclair said.

"I assume she was Caucasian?" McCain asked.

Sinclair told him she was and said the best the local police could tell, the young lady had gone missing on Halloween. She worked at a coffee stand in Enumclaw and was supposed to be home at around 11:30 p.m., after her shift Halloween night. Her roommate didn't think anything about Miller not coming home that night, because as the roommate said in the interview, 'I'm not calling her a slut or anything, but she didn't have a problem with hooking up with random guys now and again. Since it was Halloween, I just assumed she went and partied with some other friends and didn't come home. I don't keep track of her that much.'

"When she'd missed work two days in a row, her boss called the local cops," Sinclair said.

"You got her photo, I assume?" McCain asked.

"Yep," Sinclair said. "Definitely could be related to the other two. It is kind of scary how much they look alike."

McCain didn't say anything, but if Sinclair had just a little longer hair, and you looked at her from the right angle, she could definitely fit the profile too.

"So what next?" McCain asked.

"Well, now that we have the ID and a photo, we're forming a task force," she said. "It's going to get crazy real fast here in about twenty minutes. We're going to release the name and the photo to the media and we're going to shift into high gear."

"It might take a bit for the local TV reporters to put two and two together, but my guess is one of the local newspaper writers will figure out the serial killer angle pretty quickly. And once the TV folks read about it in the newspaper, they'll be all over it like a fat kid on a Twinkie."

"Yeah, we're preparing for all that," Sinclair said.

"Who's on the task force?" McCain asked.

"A forensics guy from the State Patrol in Olympia, YSO deputies Williams and Stratford, plus a detective from the Yakama Nation, and a couple detectives from the YPD. I have asked for you to be added, but I guess that's gotta go up through about eleven people in the department, and it sounds like it's a longshot."

"Well, it was nice of you to ask anyway. I don't mind staying off to the side. Sometimes you can fly under the radar and get a bit more done that way."

"As long we stay in close contact," Sinclair said. "I'm happy to share what we learn, as long as you do the same. I've appreciated all your thoughts on this one."

The next morning the headline in the *Yakima Herald-Republic* read: "CASCADE KILLER ON THE LOOSE" with the sub-head: "POSSIBLE SERIAL KILLER DUMPING BODIES IN THE MOUNTAINS WEST OF YAKIMA."

"Here we go," McCain said to Jack when he read the story. "Sinclair was right. It's about to get crazy real fast."

Jack just looked at McCain, wagged his tail about three times, and then lay back down to sleep.

The newspaper reporter had, in fact, put two and two together. It was the same reporter who had done several stories on the missing and murdered women on the Yakama Reservation. Because the reporter had worked with Sinclair on some of those stories, she had a direct line to the FBI agent.

In the story, Sinclair was quoted as saying that unfortunately, yes, they were most likely looking at one person as the killer, who seemed to be profiling women of a certain stature and hair color. The paper had printed the photos of the three murdered women, and anyone with one working eyeball could see what the stature and hair color was.

McCain figured within about three days every drug store in the county would be sold out of Miss Clairol dye-your-hair-at-home coloring kits in every color except black.

There was a large and growing population of Latinos living throughout Central Washington. Most could trace their roots to the state of Michoacán in southern Mexico, where their parents, or maybe grandparents, had been born before migrating to the United States in search of a better life.

Many of the families had found agricultural work in California, or in Texas, and as the years had gone by, they migrated north into the agricultural areas of Yakima and Wenatchee, where there was a huge need for workers in the orchards. The people found year-round jobs, pruning in the winter, thinning in the spring, and picking during the summer and fall, or else working in the many packing houses in the area where they sorted and packed apples virtually year round.

While some would go back to Mexico during the cold winters, most just stayed and continued to work. The fruit growers and warehouse operators were extremely glad to have such a hardworking supply of labor, as they would have had difficulty growing, harvesting, packing and shipping the fruit without them. Now, some 40,000 residents of the county had Hispanic surnames. And the vast majority of Hispanic women had black hair.

McCain wondered how law enforcement was ever going to protect such a huge number of potential victims. For one unfortunate woman of Mexican heritage, it was too late.

Two days later there was a story in the paper about a missing Sunnyside woman. According to Yakima Police, the twenty-two-year-old woman, Maria Jimenez, was taking summer classes at Yakima Valley College and was last seen about 7:30 at the YVC library. There was a picture of Jimenez accompanying the short story, with the police asking if anyone were to see her, to contact them.

As soon as he saw the photo, McCain called Sinclair.

"So, are your thinking this Jimenez woman might be another victim of the killer?" he asked when she answered.

"We're taking a good look at it," Sinclair explained. "I've talked to the woman's sister, and she said the girl was kind of a book worm, and never, ever came home late. After classes she called her sister and told her she was going to go to the college library to study."

Sinclair said YPD was doing all the obvious things, including checking for her car, talking to people in her classes, and looking at the video footage from the security cameras on campus.

"But if she stopped for gas, or at some fast food place, she could have met up with anyone," Sinclair said. "I've got a gut feeling that this is the work of our guy. I hope she phones her sister and tells her she decided to go with a classmate to the Tri-Cities to visit a sick grandma or something. But my guess is it isn't going to happen."

McCain, unfortunately, agreed.

"Well, there's not much I can do to help in town," McCain said. "If it is the killer, he's going to take the body to the mountains. I know it's a needle in a haystack, but once I get done with some of this paperwork, I'm thinking about heading up that way."

"Okay, well I definitely appreciate your help. Holler if you think of anything else."

When McCain hung up the phone, he tried to turn his attention back to his computer and the four more reports that needed to be filed, but he couldn't concentrate. There were nearly a million acres of public land in the Cascades, a bunch of it in Yakima County. Where would he begin?

He started thinking it through. Yes, there were hundreds of square miles in the mountains of Central Washington, but only a small portion of that was accessible by roads. And, even though the killer seemed to show an almost superhuman ability to get the dead bodies away from the roads, the farthest any body had been found was the last one, the woman from Enumclaw. Her remains had been found a little over two miles off the road. That helped narrow the search a little. Still, that left who-knows-how-many hundreds of miles of old logging roads, Forest Service roads, and other two-tracks to try to cover.

McCain also thought about where the three other bodies had been found. One had been located off Highway 12, and the other two most likely were accessed via Highway 410. Earlier, both he and Sinclair had wondered why the woman who went missing last Halloween in Enumclaw had been transported all the way around Mount Rainier and was dumped off White Pass.

Then McCain remembered that sometime in late October, Chinook Pass had been closed for a couple weeks due to a big rock slide up by Government Meadows. Several elk hunters from the west side of the Cascades were ticked off because they had to drive all the way around on I-90 and I-82 to Yakima, and back up to their camps off Highway 410. Or, they had to go around Mt. Rainier and up over White Pass, and down to the "Y".

He wondered if the killer would have dropped the body somewhere off 410 had he had the chance, but because of the slide he decided to take one of the trails up the mountain off Highway 12 to save time. Maybe the killer had to be at work, or somewhere else where he'd be missed, and decided to just get rid of the body.

McCain also thought about how he would dispose of a body if it were him. He decided he would do it at night, and he would do it on a night when there was little or no moon. He looked at his phone. Tonight called for a new moon, which meant it was the darkest night of the month.

He wondered what the moons were on the nights the other women disappeared. He googled "Moon Phases" and studied a new moon chart.

"Holy crap," he said aloud.

Within a day, the dates the three other women had gone missing aligned with a new moon. He'd definitely share that with Sinclair the next time they spoke. He was only on duty until five, so he figured he'd finish his work day by running up the Yakima River to check on a few fly fishermen until it was time to knock off.

After his shift ended McCain ran home, changed clothes, grabbed Jack, jumped in his Toyota Tundra and headed up the highway toward Chinook Pass. It was his guess that the killer was dumping the bodies up there because he was familiar with the territory. He was probably a hunter, or a hiker, and knew the mountain roads and where they went.

Back in the day, before the logging on Forest Service lands slowed, the timber companies cut roads in all over the Cascades. Most connected with Forest Service roads, but others would go for a ways and then dead end at an old burned-up slash pile. If you didn't know the roads, especially in the darkest of nights, you could easily end up on a dead-end road. Not a good idea if you had a dead body in the back seat and needed to get away in a hurry.

CHAPTER 15

McCain ran up Highway 410 about fifteen miles and turned right onto Bald Mountain Road, an arterial that led up to several different Forest Service roads, including a couple that dropped back down into the Wenas. While it certainly wasn't the only road off the highway up into the mountains, McCain thought it was the most popular because it was in the best shape. He'd seen sedans and SUVs up the road plenty of times, including some sheep hunters who were up there on Cleman Mountain in a BMW sedan of all things.

He drove up the gravel road a ways, found a good turn out, and pulled over to eat the sandwich he'd packed for supper. He hopped out, let Jack out, went to the back of the truck, dropped the tailgate and jumped up to sit and eat. Normally Jack would have been off in a flash to chase chipmunks and squirrels, but the dog had more pressing matters on his mind. Right now, there was a chance for a piece of turkey out of the sandwich that smelled so good.

"You're not a hunting dog, you're a chow hound," McCain said, and gave Jack a bite of the sandwich which he immediately gobbled up without being chewed. "You didn't even taste that."

While he ate he thought more about Mr. Chad Burke. He kept forgetting to ask Sinclair the size of the boot print at the place where they found the skull and bones. And he wondered if Sinclair had asked about any other missing women around the West that might fit the same description of those that had been found in the Cascades.

While the Green River Killer's victims were mostly found along the Green River and near SeaTac Airport south of Seattle, he did dump two bodies close to Portland, Oregon. And Ted Bundy went from murdering women in Washington State to Florida where he killed several more. If the man doing the killings was new to the area, it was possible he could have killed and dumped bodies somewhere else.

The other thing the FBI was good at was putting a profiler on the case, so McCain figured they were trying to get inside the killer's head. One thing McCain knew, or thought he knew, was that the killer was possibly removing the hearts from his victims before he dumped them. The psychologists would be analyzing that one for sure.

Did the killer's first girlfriend, a slender gal with long black hair, break his heart? Was the guy saving the hearts as a memento of each woman?

He again thought of Burke and wished he knew the guy's shoe size. Something about the track at the site of the bones was of real interest to him. He'd bug Sinclair about it for sure.

Jack had been back to the truck a couple times to check on McCain, but he was off somewhere when McCain decided it was time to move on up the road. He whistled for the dog and within a minute Jack was there, ready to jump into the truck.

As daylight turned to twilight and then to dark, McCain drove up the road with Jack sitting by his side. They went about ten miles up, past Bald Mountain and on to Manastash Ridge. They got on the ridge road and found a good spot where they could watch a vast area of the country below. From there they would be able to see any headlights of vehicles coming and going on the Forest Service roads. McCain knew it would be too far and too dark to tell what kind of rig it was, but at least he'd know if there was anyone in there tonight.

He and Jack sat there until two a.m. In four hours they had seen two rigs driving the roads below. The first he saw around 11:20. McCain was almost positive it was a Jeep because its headlights were close together and high off the ground. He spotted another set of generic headlights shortly after midnight. That vehicle had come up quite a ways and then disappeared around the curve of the hill. Most likely someone heading into a camp McCain thought.

McCain and Jack were headed home, passing through Naches when he saw that the Exxon station mini-mart was open. He wasn't usually out driving around this time of night, so he didn't realize the store stayed open all night. In the summer, with lots of traffic on the highway, it must have paid off for the store to stay open 24-7.

He decided he wanted a soda, so he turned in to grab a Pepsi. He pulled up to the store, left the truck running, and ran inside. A dude with bleached blonde hair spiked into a five-inch peak running right down the center of his head was standing behind the counter looking at a car magazine.

"Hey, how's it going?" the clerk asked.

"Okay. Time for a little caffeine," McCain answered and headed to the soda fountain.

Just then Deputy Stratford walked in, went to the coffee machine, pulled a cup, and started pouring coffee into it.

McCain walked up behind the deputy and said, "Hey, Jeremy." Stratford about jumped into the next aisle.

"Wow, you're a little jumpy," McCain said. "Maybe you better make that coffee unleaded."

"No, I definitely need the caffeine," Stratford said. "I hate these graveyard shifts. What the hell are you doing up at this hour?"

"Heading over the pass to meet some friends to fish for steelhead on the Cowlitz," McCain lied. "If I'm not there, standing on the boat launch at 5 a.m., they'll leave without me."

"Sounds like good friends," the deputy said.

"So, how's the task force going?" McCain asked. "Making any headway?"

"Well, we're just getting started," Stratford explained. "I'm learning a lot from the other members. It is interesting to see how they work, and what they think about the killer."

"Yeah, I bet it is," McCain said. "Well, Jack is sitting out in my running truck, so I best be on my way. Good luck on catching that guy."

"Thanks. Good luck fishing."

On his way back to the counter McCain grabbed a PayDay candy bar to go with his soda, paid for the items, and walked out to the truck. He opened the PayDay and ate a bite while two big brown eyes watched every move he made. Finally, when the candy bar was down to one bite, he gave it to Jack. The dog swallowed it in one big gulp.

"I coulda just fed you a rock and you wouldn't have known the difference," he said to the dog that wasn't paying any attention. He was snarfling around the seat in hopes that a peanut had fallen for him to lick up.

"You're a goofy dog, but I love you anyway," McCain said, rubbing the dog's ears as he backed out of the parking spot. He had waited until Stratford was gone, so he could head in the opposite direction of the Cowlitz River, toward his air-conditioned house and his very comfortable bed.

CHAPTER 16

The killer had been feeling the heat. Not just the incessant heat of the late July days, but the fire inside to satisfy something that had been burning in him for most of his life. He hated that bitch. She needed to die. They were all bitches who didn't care about him.

He had watched the moons and knew it was time so he went on a hunt. He'd spotted the Mexican girl walking into the YVC parking lot toward a handful of cars parked there. She was perfect. Fairly tall, slender with long black hair. She walked to a white Honda and climbed in. She left the parking lot, turned left on Nob Hill and headed out to I-82. He followed a ways behind as she merged onto the freeway and headed south toward the Lower Valley.

When she was down the freeway a few miles he pulled up alongside of her and waited for her to look at him. When she did, he pointed at her tire with some urgency. It worked almost every time. She pulled over, and he pulled in behind her. Being on the freeway wasn't ideal. Other times he had been on quiet rural roads. But if he was careful it would work. He watched the traffic and when there was a break he jumped out. She had already gotten out and was checking her tires when he came from behind and punched her, hard in the face. It always stunned them enough that he could then overpower them.

He caught her as she was falling, dragged her to the backseat of his rig and quickly put zip ties around her wrists and ankles. He put duct tape around her mouth and laid her in the seat where she couldn't be seen.

He waited for traffic to clear in both directions again, and then drove her car down the embankment, through the barbed wire siding fence and into a bunch of brush next to the Yakima River. From the freeway it was almost impossible to see the car, and it might be fall when the leaves all dropped before anyone did. Even if someone got real nosy about the break in the fence, it would still take a while he told himself.

He wiped the steering wheel, the knob on the shifter, and the door handles and then walked back up to his car, jumped in and was gone.

It wasn't the ideal place for what he did, but he was positive no one had paid any attention to the guy helping a disabled motorist.

He was living in a crappy double wide mobile home out in Terrace Heights. Way out past the county landfill with no neighbors within two miles. That's where he took them. And that's where he took her. He loved to see the fear in their eyes. And when they saw the hatred he had for them they even got more frightened.

He didn't make them suffer for long. He would yell at them and tell them how much he hated them until he couldn't scream anymore. Then he would strangle them with his bare hands. And when he was sure they were dead he would use his hunting knife to cut open their chest and rip out their heart.

The next day he would put the heart in a plastic garbage bag, put it in with the rest of his trash and drop it by the landfill as he was going to work. Later that night he would load the body in the back of his rig and drive up into the mountains to set them free.

Some of the bodies he would pack over his shoulder. On others he had used his game cart to wheel them out away from the roads. He never knew where he was going to set them free, but he always knew when he saw it, even in the almost pitch dark.

When he woke up the next morning, he saw the news that the idiots in the sheriff's office had finally figured out that the killings were done by the same person. Duh! They still hadn't made the connection to Colorado though. They really were stupid. But sooner or later someone would check around and they'd know these weren't his only victims.

Maybe he'd head to someplace new. Or maybe he'd stick around to see just how close they might come. Maybe he'd find another victim. Maybe not.

I t was going to be a hot one. McCain could already feel the heat creeping in through the east-facing windows, and it wasn't even nine o'clock yet. It had been a late night, and he would probably still be sleeping if Jack hadn't awakened him to go out to pee.

He switched on the TV as he ate some cereal and watched Wendy Storm giving the weather forecast. She was the nighttime weather person but was filling in for the normal morning person, or so she said. Wendy confirmed what McCain already knew: it was going to be Africa-hot out there again today. She signed off by saying, "stay cool out there, that's the weather, I'm Wendy Storm."

McCain said, "I shit you not."

He had the next three days off, so today McCain thought he would go up and do a little more snooping around in the mountains. He had seen that vehicle go up the road below him last night, or more correctly, earlier this morning. He thought it might have been a camper making a late arrival, but he wanted to check it out anyway. And he wanted to look around the Wenas side of the hill too.

Before he got going, he called Sinclair.

"Hey, McCain," she said in a tone of voice he had not heard before.

"If this is not a good time, we can talk later," he said.

"The stuff is really hitting the fan today. I've got about five hundred calls on my desk from people who think they know who the killer is. And a bunch more from people who are worried their daughter or friend or sister could be next, because they look just like the three murdered women."

"Well—" he started before she cut him off.

"And besides the local news people, all of sudden I've got calls from TV stations and reporters from Seattle and Portland. I even had a call from a reporter from *The New York Times*."

"Wow, bad news travels fast. I won't bug you now, but I do have a couple of thoughts and questions."

"I'm about to go into a task force meeting. Can we talk later?"

"Sure, just call me when it works for you." And he hung up.

He wanted to talk to Sinclair before he headed to the mountains, so he decided to wait for her call closer to home. Needing to kill a little time while staying in phone service range, he decided to go down to the river. Every now and again he'd grab Austin Meyers, and he and Jack and the kid would go do a little fishing. This was the perfect time to do so. He called the Meyers' phone and Austin answered.

"Hi, Luke. Are you hunting for the Cascade Killer?"

"Naw, the FBI is handling that. In fact, Jack and I are going fishing on the river in a few and wanted to see if you wanted to come along?"

"Sure!" Austin said. "I'm totally bored. Let me check with my mom."

Austin was knocking on McCain's door ten minutes later. He had his spinning rod in his hand and an old-fashioned creel over his shoulder. He was in shorts, a Russell Wilson number 3 Seahawks t-shirt and was wearing a Boston Red Sox ball cap.

"Did you bring any food or water?" McCain asked.

"Yeah, my mom fixed a couple of peanut butter sandwiches for us, and I have a bottle of Mountain Dew."

"Okay, well, let me grab my gear and we'll be on our way."

McCain knew that fishing the river during mid-morning was probably not going to be the most productive time of day, but even then he figured they'd catch a fish or two. And, because Austin's dad lived in Arizona and didn't get up here much after he had divorced the boy's mother, the only time he got to go fishing was when McCain took him.

They'd fished before, and McCain had helped Austin through a hunter's safety course in January, so he could get his hunting license this fall. And he'd gone to a few of the boy's Pony league baseball games the past couple of months.

"You think the FBI is going to catch the killer?" Austin asked as they walked down the trail to the river.

"Yes, I do," said McCain. "They always do. Sooner or later the person makes a mistake, and they get caught. The challenge is going to be trying to catch him before he kills any more women."

"Yeah, I sure hope they do. Do you think they'll want Jack to help again?"

"I don't know. Probably not, but they could."

When Jack heard his name, his ears perked up and he looked up at Austin.

The boy scratched Jack's back and said, "I sure hope so. It was so cool how he tracked the bear to where that one woman was."

"Don't start pumping him up too much," McCain said. "He's already getting a big head."

When they hit the river, Jack took off downstream, splashing and playing and drinking water from the river. McCain and Austin went upstream to the first deep hole where McCain knew the bigger trout liked to lay.

"Throw your spinner over toward those bigger rocks and let it roll down through the hole," McCain instructed.

Austin followed the directions perfectly, and within a few seconds he was fighting a nice fat rainbow.

"Way to go! Do you want to keep it for dinner?" McCain asked.

"Let's let it go. That way I can catch it again maybe sometime."

"Good idea."

As they fished along upriver, McCain and Austin talked.

"How's your baseball team doing?" McCain asked.

"Okay. We've won four and lost three. I got a triple the other day."

About then Jack came running along the edge of the water. The dog was sopping wet, and as he got to McCain and the boy, he stopped and started shaking the water off.

"HEY!" Austin yelled, holding his hands up in front of his face to try to shield it from the dog-water assault.

McCain just laughed.

"I'd sure like to have a dog like Jack someday," Austin said as he wiped water from his arms and legs.

"Well, keep getting good grades and showing your mom you're responsible enough to take care of a dog, and I bet she'll let you have one. When it is time, I'll help you find a good one."

"That'd be cool. Maybe you can help me train him to become a tracking dog, just like Jack."

"I'd like that. And so would Jack. How about we dig into those sandwiches?"

As they sat on a rock and ate the peanut butter and jelly sandwiches, they talked about dogs and girls and football. All kinds of guy stuff. And as they did, a yellow dog sat right in front of them, watching every bite they took. Austin was the first to give in. He tore off some crust to give to Jack who happily gobbled it up and waited for more.

"You are one spoiled dog," McCain said. "If a stranger saw you acting like that, they'd think you never got fed."

Austin just laughed and gave Jack another bite of bread.

The two fished for a while longer and then headed back to the house.

"Thanks for taking me fishing," Austin said. "It was fun. You'll probably have to tell my mom about the big one I caught and let go, because she might not believe me."

"Tell her to call me. And thanks for going with me. Jack's fun, but he's not much for conversation. We'll do it again soon."

With that, Austin said goodbye, gave a wave and headed home.

A short time later, as McCain was getting geared up to head to the mountains, Sinclair called back.

"Sorry about that," she said, still sounding stressed. "My boss is all over me about this serial killer deal. He wants to see some progress. Like I don't?"

"I just have a question or two, and a couple thoughts. We can talk later if that helps."

"No, sorry," she said. "The woman from Sunnyside is still missing, which really has me worried. We haven't found her vehicle. And everything else seems to be a dead end, including the check on the places that rent horses. No one of interest rented any horses during the times the other women went missing."

"Anything on the boot photo I took up on the trail where the bones were found?"

"The crime lab people said it was most likely from a man's shoe or boot, size 12 or maybe 12 and a half. But they couldn't tell from the photo if the track was three months or three years old."

"Alright, well, holler if there's anything I can do to help."

"Just talking to you helps," she said, her voice softening. "Something about you does that to me. I'm just getting so frustrated."

"I totally understand," he said, because he didn't know what else to say.

"So, what have you been up to since we last talked?" she asked.

"Oh, you know, just watching over about a thousand anglers from here to Cle Elum. Pretty taxing duty."

He hoped that would lighten her mood a little.

Then he said, "Actually, after work last night Jack and I ran up into the Manastash on a whim. I figured if this guy had taken another victim, he might be dumping the body back up off Highway 410 somewhere. It's big country, but we had nothing better to do. Jack chased squirrels, and I watched for crazy dudes."

"Find any?"

"Just three. I water-boarded them, and no matter how much I tried, I couldn't get them to talk. Then I remembered, oh yeah, squirrels can't talk. I started thinking about when the killer might have dumped the bodies. We're guessing he does it at night, but I thought he might be picking the darkest of nights, where there is a new moon."

"Okay," she said. "Go on."

"I've spent a lot of nights in the woods, and on the night of a new moon it is so dark even the animals are affected. So I started looking at the moon phases. Guess when the last new moon was?"

"Two nights ago? When the Jimenez woman went missing?"

"Actually, it was last night. That's why I went up into the mountains to see what I could see."

"Damn," she said. She paused to think for a few seconds and said, "Don't believe what everyone else says, you are smarter than you look, Luke McCain. "

"Aw, shucks," he said.

"Wait a minute, wasn't there a lawman on one of those old westerns on TV named Luke McCain? I remember watching it in re-runs with my dad."

"I have no idea what you are talking about. You must be WAY older than me, because I don't remember any of those old TV shows."

"I'll think of it," she said, ignoring his little jab. "Now, I gotta go catch a killer. You have fun harassing anglers."

McCain called Jack, went out to his truck, fired it up, turned the AC to max and was about to take off when his phone chimed. *Why did WSU disband its water polo team? Their horses all drowned.* It was followed by about nine happy faces laughing so hard tears were coming out of their eyes.

It wasn't that funny, McCain thought. Especially not to the horses.

McCain, with Jack riding shotgun, motored west on Highway 12 toward the mountains. As he slowed to go through Naches, he looked closely at the cars sitting at the fruit stands, stores, restaurants, mini-marts and finally the hardware store on the west end of the strip that was now the retail part of the town.

Naches was like a thousand other small towns in America. It had been a quaint little town back in the 50s and 60s, where everyone from the farms and orchards in the area would come to shop for groceries, eat at a restaurant, and go to church. But then in the late 60s the state built a new highway next to the river, bypassing the town. With the advent of newer, faster, more reliable cars, people started doing their shopping in the much bigger city of Yakima, fifteen miles down the road. Businesses in Naches started drying up, and the ones that survived picked up and moved out to the new highway, where all the traffic was.

Today there was an array of assorted businesses on each side of the highway and especially during the busy tourist time, they made hay. McCain didn't see much of interest as he drove through the businesses until he spotted the silver Honda in the parking lot of the hardware store. He immediately felt the urge to buy some six-penny nails.

McCain pulled into the hardware parking lot, parked, and as he had been doing for most of the past month when he had Jack with him, either in his state truck or in his Tundra, he left the rig running with the AC on and the doors locked.

"I'll be right back," he said to the dog, like Jack knew how to keep time, and headed into the store.

The hardware store was a typical for a small town. It served orchardists and homeowners in the area with items they needed. It also had a decent fishing section, with rods, reels, and a variety of lures and baits the local anglers used on the rivers and lakes in the Cascades. McCain was a frequent customer, so he knew the proprietor and some of the main workers.

"Hey Luke," the owner said when he saw him come through the door. "Off duty today, eh?"

"Yeah, I'm working on a couple projects," he fibbed as his eyes searched the store for Chad Burke.

"Well, let me know if you need any help," the store owner said.

McCain wandered down a main aisle, scanning up and down the other aisles until he found Burke in the small section that carried camping supplies.

When he saw McCain, Burke said, "Hey, I don't think they serve ice cream here."

"Oh, right," McCain said, acting like he didn't recognize Burke for a minute. "You're the guy with my dream jobs. How are the fish biting on the Yakima?"

"Fishing's been good," Burke said. "Best late in the day."

"The whitewater deal should be kicking in pretty soon," McCain said.

"We'll be running trips starting right after Labor Day," Burke said. "Have you ever done it?"

"Once on the Deschutes River down by Bend," McCain answered. "But it was pretty tame."

"Stop by when we get going. I'll get you on a boat if you're interested."

"Looks like you're going to be doing a little camping," McCain observed dumbly.

"Yeah, I have a little work to do in the mountains," Burke said, then turned and headed to the cashier's counter.

McCain was afraid to push it too much. He grabbed a handful of Rooster Tails off the pegs in the fishing aisle, one aisle over, and then also headed to the counter.

Burke looked at the lures and said to McCain, "I thought you were a fly guy?"

"Oh, I'll fish with lures now and again, but these are for my neighbor kid. He lost five of these this morning fishing with me on the Naches. I'll make him work them off by taking care of my spoiled dog."

"Well, good luck," Burke said, and he headed for the door.

"Yeah, catch you later," McCain said as he concentrated on Burke's boots and their tread. If he wasn't mistaken, they were about a size 12, maybe 13.

McCain had the urge to follow Burke, but he also wanted to get back up near Bald Mountain to do some checking around. He decided he'd go west up 410, to the Bald Mountain Road turnoff, and if it happened that Burke was going that way too, well, so be it.

Burke was about a half mile ahead of him, so McCain stayed back and just watched. It was short lived, however. Burke turned left at the Y and headed up toward White Pass. McCain thought about following, but he decided he'd go ahead and go back up by Manastash Ridge where he'd seen the rig around midnight.

He was in no hurry, so he took his time driving up the Forest Service road past Bald Mountain on the way to the ridge. He was on the same road as the night before, and he followed it along until he hit a road that gradually turned west off the main road up to the ridge. He was pretty sure this was the road the second rig had driven up in the dark.

All these roads saw a surprising amount of traffic in the summer. Several jeep clubs would camp down along the river, and they'd come up here and drive around all day. McCain failed to see the appeal of just driving around on dirt roads all day, by the jeepers or the road-hunters in the fall, but that was probably because he had to do it as part of his job.

Today, though, he was on a different mission. He was looking for a place where someone might have pulled off and walked down from the road a ways. He drove slowly, watching closely for anything that might tell him what that rig had been doing up there the night before.

Yes, the person driving the rig might have been coming in late to a camp. And if he found a camp up here, he'd stop and ask the campers about that. Unfortunately, he found none, and he started getting a really bad feeling in his gut.

CHAPTER 17

McCain threw the Toyota into first gear and let the vehicle creep along as he searched for any tire tracks, shoe prints or some other clue along the road that might tell him more about the vehicle he'd seen the night before. He also looked ahead, occasionally turning off the road to check all the obvious flat spots where someone might have had a camp recently.

The road was dusty and hot and seemed desolate. No birds chirped. No chipmunks skittered across the road. It was weird, he thought.

McCain drove around a big bend in the road and finally he saw life. But it wasn't the living things he was hoping to see. A flock of turkey vultures was circling a small canyon downhill from the road. They circled and circled, like a scene from an old western. Clearly, they were zeroing in on something dead. Yes, it could have been a deer or calf elk killed by a cougar. Or, he reasoned, it could be a human body, dumped down the hill in the trees by a serial killer in the dark of the new moon.

From his years of experience in the field, McCain knew turkey vultures were among the most proficient of all the scavengers.

Sometimes the big birds would spot their meals from the air, but more often than not turkey vultures smelled the dead animals they ended up scavenging. McCain had read that the birds have an unbelievable sense of smell and can scent carrion from over a mile away. He decided to see what this group of vultures smelled.

McCain parked as close to the circling birds as he could. He loaded his pack with water, trail mix, flagging tape and a jacket, and headed for the vultures riding the currents in a big loop. He kept Jack close to him, as he didn't want the dog chasing a rabbit through somebody's fresh tracks or any other evidence if he happened to find a body. Around his neck with an elastic harness he wore his binoculars, and he stopped to look through them often, searching for colors that didn't match the natural surroundings, or any unusual disturbances in the foliage or the ground ahead.

When McCain had walked roughly three-quarters of a mile he spotted a thin, indented line in the dirt about thirty yards ahead. At first, he thought someone had ridden a mountain bike through the rocks and shrubs and trees. But as he got a closer look, the tire track was too thin to be a mountain bike. Mountain bike tires are fat so that they can go over rough ground easier. This track was more like that made by a racing bike tire.

Would anyone ride a ten-speed out through this stuff, McCain wondered. He didn't think so. Then it dawned on him. He'd seen those tracks during hunting season. Some hunters used game carts to haul out deer or elk quarters on the thin-tired carts so they didn't have to carry the meat on their backs. He leaned closer and could see the tread pattern in places, meaning the tracks were relatively fresh. Old tracks would have been smudged by the wind and rain.

Keeping Jack at heel, McCain followed the tracks, carefully staying to one side so as not to disturb them. As he continued, he found a few partial footprints. Wherever he found them he tied a piece of the bright pink flagging tape to the nearest bush or tree. Sometimes the tire tracks would disappear on the hardest ground or over rock, but by staying on the same general course, McCain would eventually pick the track up again.

It took him almost a half hour to cover the next mile. When the track finally ended up at the body of Maria Jimenez, McCain was saddened, but not surprised.

Evidently the vultures had just found the body because they had done very little damage. The gaping cut in the chest, on the other hand, and the bruises around the woman's throat revealed the fatal damage done by the killer. McCain had been right. The killer was taking the heart out of the bodies before he dumped them.

McCain wasn't a terribly religious man, but he said a prayer for this poor woman, or girl, really. Just twenty-two. A tragedy for sure. With the flagging tape he carefully circled the body in a ten-foot arc. Then, as he had done at the body found by Jack, he took his sweaty t-shirt off, and draped it over a bush as close to the body as he could in hopes that his human scent would keep the scavengers away.

He put on his jacket, told Jack to heel, and started back toward the truck, careful not to disturb any tracks. At the truck, he saw his phone had no service, so he drove back up to Manastash Ridge and called Sinclair.

"What's up?" she asked.

"I've found the Jimenez girl's body."

"What? How?"

"I need you and the sheriff and whoever else up here as soon as possible. It's definitely the missing girl, and it was definitely done by the same guy. I think I've got boot tracks."

"Tell me where you are and how to get there, and someone will be there as quickly as possible."

He figured the YSO deputies knew how to get there, but he gave her the coordinates from his GPS unit just in case.

"I just missed him, Sara," he said quietly. "I know it was still too late for the girl, but I was that close. I watched him drive by last night. I should have followed the lights."

It was the first time he'd called her by her first name. She knew he was hurting when he said it.

"You couldn't have known, Luke. We'll talk about it later. I'll get there as quickly as I can."

The first deputy to arrive was Paul Garcia. He'd been at the first site the night Jack had backtracked the bear, but McCain hadn't remembered him being at the other bodies, at least not when he had been there.

"Thanks for coming so quickly," McCain said as Garcia climbed out of his marked SUV.

"Yeah, no problem," Garcia said. "The lady FBI agent was going to catch a ride with Williams, or maybe Stratford. She was worried her car wouldn't make it up here. They should be here in ten."

"Okay, we'll wait," McCain said.

Jack went over to Garcia who gave him a few pats on the side. "How in the hell did you find the body so quickly?" Garcia asked. "Did Jack find her?"

"No, Jack just kept me company. I spotted some turkey vultures and went in to see what they were working on. It's a day off, and I thought what the heck, Jack needed some exercise and I wanted to do some elk scouting, so we headed up this way," McCain said, with a little creative editing included.

"What are the odds?" Garcia asked, skeptically. "You've been around when every one of these bodies have been found."

"Yeah, well, I do work up here in the mountains a lot," McCain said. "So I seem to be around. And let me think about it. Oh yeah, that's right, it is you guys who called me in on the other three."

Deputy Williams arrived without Sinclair and expressed surprise that she and Stratford weren't there already. "They were ahead of me," he said. "They should have been here by now."

All three men looked back down the road, like Sinclair and Stratford would just magically appear, coming their way. Garcia went to his rig and radioed Stratford, who replied a minute later, saying that they were on their way. He'd taken the wrong turn.

A few minutes later, Stratford's SUV came bouncing up the road in a cloud of dust. Sinclair and Stratford exited the vehicle as Williams fixed Stratford with a stern look.

"How can you get lost?" Williams asked Stratford. "You're up in this country all the time. Did you not hear the words Bald Mountain Road when the call came in?"

"Yeah, I did," Stratford said. "But I got mixed up and turned up the Rock Creek Road."

"It's no big deal," Sinclair said. "We're here now. So, Officer McCain, can you lead us to the body, and as we go, tell us how you discovered it?"

McCain looked at her shoes and was pleasantly surprised to see that she wore hiking boots. He again shouldered his daypack and whistled for Jack who came and fell in line with the group.

"The coroner is on the way too," Sinclair said. "One of the deputies can come back up and wait for them after he sees where the body is."

After they had walked down the hill a good ways, McCain pointed out the thin tire track and a couple of the shoe prints he had marked. A little farther down the hill, he stopped and said, "See the pink circle of tape down there in the brush? That is where the body is."

"Okay," Sinclair said. "I don't think we all need to be down there. And one of you deputies needs to go back to the rigs to meet the coroner. Another deputy can stay here. McCain, I'd like you to come along with me and, I assume, Deputy Williams?"

Williams was the ranking deputy, so he said, "Stratford, you're way younger and fitter than Deputy Garcia. Why don't you hike back to the rigs, and Paul, you stay here per the agent's request."

"I'm fine with that," Stratford said as he turned and headed back the other direction. "Those dead bodies give me the willies."

Sinclair, Williams, McCain and Jack hiked down the last 500 yards to the body. When they arrived, McCain and Williams stood back and let the FBI agent do her thing. She carefully got in close to the body and examined it without touching it. And then she took out her camera and took about a hundred photos.

"Did you notice anything here, McCain?" she asked after looking at the body and surrounding area.

"Other than the gaping chest wound and the big space where the heart should be, I did notice bruising around her throat. And it looks like she was bound around the wrists. I couldn't see the ankles. And she had a fairly large bruise forming on the left side of her face. It's hard to see from here, but I looked from down below and I could see it."

"Okay, I'll check it out," she said. "I'm just guessing here, but I don't think she was sexually assaulted. She's in the same clothes her sister said she was wearing the day she went missing. Would someone re-dress a body if there was a sexual component to this thing?"

"How do you know?" Williams said. "This guy obviously has some serious issues."

They looked and chatted for a few more minutes and then heard some voices up the hill. It was the coroner's crew talking to Garcia. They were packing a stretcher and some other equipment. It was going to get real crowded here in a couple minutes, so McCain took the opportunity to bow out. He told

Sinclair that unless she needed him here, he was going to head back up to the truck.

"That's fine," she said and paused. "You know, you could do one more thing for me. If you don't mind, can you try to follow the wheel track back up the hill? That would get us to where the killer parked. Maybe we can get a truck or car tire track there."

McCain did just that. At first, he tried to follow the track that would have been made by the cart without the added weight of the woman, when the killer would have been pushing it back to a vehicle. Then he realized that was stupid. The deeper tire imprint was easier to follow, and it had to come from the vehicle too. So he followed it instead.

When he got to the road, sure enough McCain could see where a vehicle had pulled off into the grass. The problem was it was very rocky, so tire imprints were incredibly hard to see. McCain again pulled some pink flagging tape out of his pack and tied it to a bush nearby. He'd leave it to the experts to see if they could get an imprint of the tire. But from what he could see, they were going to have a tough time.

All this time, Jack had been the perfect dog, sitting quietly off to the side and dutifully following McCain wherever he went. As they were walking back to his truck, McCain turned and said to Jack, "Hey boy! You've been such a good dog, let's go find a squirrel."

Jack took off for the trees. As McCain followed, he noticed something small and white in the long grass. He reached down to pick it up. It was one of those wrappers that individually wrapped toothpicks came in. It was empty, but on the outside McCain could read the name of a restaurant. The paper was still white and clean, so McCain figured it hadn't been there long. Then he looked back to his pink marking tape. He was quite a ways from where the vehicle had been parked. Too far, in his opinion, for something to have blown out of a rig. Especially last night. There was absolutely no wind when he and Jack were sitting on the ridge watching for cars.

He decided he would give it to Sinclair to see if she wanted to follow up on it.

McCain and Jack hiked around a bit more, and then went back to where the truck and the other official rigs were parked. They waited there for Sinclair to see if she had learned anything else.

When she arrived, she asked if she could catch a ride back to town with him.

"Sure," he said. "Jump in."

He told Jack to get in the backseat, gave a nod to the deputies standing at their cars, and they were on their way.

"I can't tell you how much I appreciate you finding the girl, and doing it on your own time."

"No problem. I just had a hunch about the new moon thing and was lucky to pick the road the killer used."

"I don't know. Your hunches have seemed to be right on."

"I'm still mad at myself for not checking out the lights that came in here last night. I might have caught the killer, or at least might have been able to identify his vehicle."

"How could you know?" she asked. "You couldn't."

"I'm sure you are checking on this, but are there any women fitting the description of the dead women who have gone missing or found dead in any other states?"

"Yes, I sent out that request a couple days ago. I've heard from some, and they don't have anything that might be related. I'm still waiting on a couple others."

McCain reached into his shirt pocket. "Look at this. I found it not too far from the place where the killer parked his rig. Might be worth checking out."

Sinclair took the little toothpick wrapper and looked it over. "Antonio's? Do you know the place?"

"Yeah, it is a nice steakhouse on Yakima Avenue. Has a pretty nice bar too. It's one of the popular night spots in town."

"That shows you how much I get out. I've never been there."

"I've been a couple times with some buddies, but as you know, doing the bar scene is not really my thing."

"Well, if the killer frequents the place, we can at least check it out. But with no description of the guy, how do we even know who to ask about?"

"Unless you need to be someplace right away, we could swing by Antonio's now. That way you can at least say you've seen the place."

"Yeah, I'd be up for that. What about Jack?"

"We're going right by my place. Let me drop him off and feed him, and we'll be on our way."

"Sounds good. I'd like to see where the famous Luke McCain lives."

"Believe me, it's not terribly exciting. But Jack and I get along just fine there."

"Not to get too personal, but how does a good-looking guy with a good job and an average sense of humor not have a significant other?"

"Agent Sinclair, how would I . . . wait, you are asking about me, aren't you?" he said with a smile.

She just stared at him.

"I know this sounds corny, but I just haven't met the right girl, I guess. I lived with a woman when I was working on the west side of the state, but she had some issues that didn't become evident until she was firmly entrenched in my house. And I've dated a few ladies over the past few years, but nothing has really hit the 'this is her' button."

He looked at her, and she was looking back with a goofy grin on her face.

"What about you?" McCain asked. "How come an above-average looking lady with some smarts and, how'd you put it, an average sense of humor, isn't married?"

"I got very close once. But the shithead decided it would be fun to have a little weekend fling with his ex-girlfriend. I'm an FBI agent, don't you think I might find this out? On a whim, I did a little checking right before our wedding day and learned of his unfaithfulness. How's the old saying go? Once burned, twice shy. Or is it once bitten, twice shy? Doesn't matter, you get the point."

"Understandable. Well, let me be honest with you. I think you're very attractive, and once we get beyond this whole serial killer thing, I'd like to get to know you better. That is if you'd be interested."

"Funny, I've been having the same thoughts. But let's do get this asshole caught before we travel down the getting-to-know-you-better road."

They talked a bit more about the girl, the turkey vultures, the game cart, and the human tracks.

"You think the boot tracks will match the partial track that I found up with the bones of the Miller woman?" McCain asked.

"I don't know, but it wouldn't surprise me. The crime scene people will definitely check it."

A few minutes later they were pulling into his place. McCain climbed out of the truck and let Jack out the back door.

"Come on in," he said to Sinclair. "I think all my dirty shorts and socks have been kicked under the bed. It will only take me a few minutes to feed Jack, and then we can be on our way."

"You might want to wash your face and put on a clean shirt," Sinclair said. "You look like you've been wrestling with a cougar."

"Will do. I wouldn't want to embarrass you," he said and laughed.

McCain fed Jack, who wolfed his kibble down like it was the best tasting food he'd ever eaten. Then he freshened up, put on a pair of clean Wranglers and a Polo shirt, combed his dark brown hair and declared himself ready.

When they got to Antonio's, the place was jumping. The music coming over the sound system was fairly loud, and the crowd noises made it even more difficult to hear.

"You want to grab a table?" McCain asked. "I can get you a drink."

"You know what, let me look around for a bit, just to get a good idea what this place is, and who the clientele is, and then let's go someplace else."

"You got it."

When they got back to McCain's truck, he said, "I have a nice spring salmon fillet in my refrigerator. I was going to barbecue it tonight. I'd be happy to share it with you. It would definitely be nice to have some company. That is if you can stand a yellow Lab watching you eat."

She laughed and said, "I'd love it. Run me to my car at the sheriff's office, and I'll follow you home."

McCain grilled the salmon on the barbecue, threw a quick salad together, warmed some garlic French bread in the oven, and they ate on the patio. He made Jack lay down while they ate, so neither of them had to put up with hungry brown eyes staring at them.

"That was really good," Sinclair said when they were finished.

"I caught the salmon with my own two hands," he said. "It's my favorite fish to catch and to eat."

"You won't get any argument from me. I guess I can add one more quality to your list. Looks, good job, kinda funny, and you can cook. Why aren't the ladies beating your door down?"

"Don't get too excited. Salmon's about the only thing I can make that tastes good. And, I think you could cook a spring salmon in the dishwasher, and it would eat just fine. Sorry, I don't have any dessert."

"No problem. I really need to get going. Tomorrow is going to be another crazy day, now that you've found the Jimenez girl."

McCain and Jack stood on the porch and watched her drive away.

"I really would like to get to know her better," he said to the yellow dog before turning in to clean up the dishes.

CHAPTER 18

The killer was amazed the body of the girl had been found so quickly. Someone had been very lucky. Still, it was scary to think that the idiots would have been there just hours after he had set the woman free. He had always had the help of the elements to cover his tire tracks and footprints. He had used the game cart a couple times before, when the terrain allowed, and because it was a quicker way to get in and out of where he had let her go.

There was no word about the white car he dumped by the river. That was good. They wouldn't find it until fall, if at all. Not that he was worried about that because he had wiped down the car inside and out.

They also knew now about the heart. Again, that didn't matter. So what? He removed the bitches' hearts. What did that tell anyone?

Still, it was a close call. The closest yet. He would have to be a little more careful from now on.

He would wait. If he could. Until the heat and anger rose up in him again. At that point he could make no promises.

It had been three days since McCain found the body, and the media was going bonkers over it. A fourth body in the killing spree that even the national news was now calling the Cascade Killer. McCain had seen Sinclair interviewed on TV a couple of times, and the *Yakima Herald-Republic* had run a series of in-depth stories about the four victims, including a timeline of when they disappeared and a map of where their bodies had been located

Luckily for McCain, Sinclair had kept his name out of the news as the person who had discovered the body. She told reporters that a hiker had seen the vultures and went to see what they were circling over. The next time he talked to her he would have to thank her for that.

Maria Jimenez had been positively identified by her sister after her body had arrived at the county morgue. Later the coroner would announce that she had been strangled to death. There was no evidence of a sexual attack. The only other physical evidence was the bruising on the left side of her face. The woman had been hit prior to being killed, the coroner reported.

The crime scene crew had taken plaster imprints of the tire tracks and the few partial shoe tracks that McCain had found. They weren't quite ready to say the tire tracks came from a game cart, but McCain was positive they were. He'd seen too many on his checks of hunters over the years. When they did determine that it was a game cart, maybe then they could figure out who manufactured it based on the details of the track. That might lead them to some purchase records if the cart was bought direct from the factory or through some online store.

The investigation was moving along, but at glacial speed, McCain thought. The killer was either very smart or very lucky. Probably both.

On the following Monday, McCain decided it was about time to follow up on the Johnson boys. It was his experience that arresting poachers for one offense rarely stopped them from breaking the game laws again. The police arrest records were full of people who habitually took game and fish out of season.

With the tables in the Yakima County Jail now securely bolted to the floor, LeRoy Johnson Sr. seemed to be firmly incarcerated. LeRoy Junior and his brother Theodore, on the other hand, were out in the world, most likely causing trouble. The brothers struck McCain as the types who might enjoy doing a little hunting out of season.

The Johnsons' house in Tieton was closer than Teddy Johnson's Cle Elum cabin, so McCain ran up to the old man's place first. He slowed as he approached the driveway. Surprisingly, the house was a regular beehive of activity. The flock of chickens was back, with birds scratching and pecking everywhere. McCain saw Junior's Chevy and Teddy's Dodge sitting in the gravel driveway.

A couple half-breed dogs were tied by a length of chain to two trees next to the house. They both strained at the chains, barking at the chickens. Or more likely, McCain thought, they were just barking to hear their heads rattle. It always amazed him how people could just let their dogs bark incessantly. Didn't it get on their nerves? Even trying to watch television, listening to the dogs bark in the background would drive him nuts.

There was nobody outside, so he decided to cruise up the driveway and see if anyone popped their head outside. Sure enough, he had barely stopped when LeRoy Junior stepped out on the porch. McCain saw him turn and say something to someone inside, and a second later a thinner version of the younger Johnson stepped out. Williams had been right. They were definitely kicked by the same mule.

The brothers were the same height, had the same round face, and had the same wispy bit of sandy-colored hair on top of their heads, which was forecasting some serious male-pattern baldness in their future. While LeRoy Junior was kind of dumpy, Teddy was in pretty good shape. He looked like one of those guys who hadn't worked out or lifted a weight a day in his life, but he was strong in a natural sort of way. His brother missed that gene, along with a few others, evidently. The men were outfitted in jeans and t-shirts, LeRoy in a blue Seattle Mariners shirt, and Teddy in a black shirt with some kind of a logo on it. Probably from a rock band that nobody had ever heard of, McCain figured.

He got out of the truck and tried to say hello over the barking dogs, without much success.

"Unless you got a warrant, you can just get the hell outta here," Teddy hollered.

"Just wanted to stop by and see how LeRoy was doing. I know he's pretty close to your father, and I wanted to make sure he was doing okay."

"Well, ain't that benevolent of ya," Teddy said. "My brother's doin' just fine, thank you. Now git outta here."

"Okay, well, you boys have a good day," McCain said as he began backpedaling for his truck. As he passed Teddy's pickup he glanced into the bed and spotted a thin-wheeled game cart and what appeared to be fresh blood.

"Next time, save yourself a trip and send a postcard," Teddy said before he and LeRoy returned to the house.

As McCain backed out of the driveway the dogs were still barking and the chickens, about thirty of them, were picking and scratching, scurrying around like a bunch of ants.

There were about fourteen reasons why Teddy Johnson might have a game cart in the back of his truck, McCain thought. But in the middle of summer, combined with fresh blood stains, only about three of those reasons were likely legitimate. He had no reason to think Teddy might be involved with the dead bodies in the Cascades, but it certainly was a strange coincidence. More realistically, Teddy and his simple brother had picked up where the old man had left off.

Even so, McCain decided to call Hargraves and let him know what he had seen.

"Hey Luke, what's up?" Hargraves asked.

"On a whim I ran up to the LeRoy Johnson compound today. You'll never guess what I saw."

"I don't know, a bear riding a bike."

"Nope. Before they ran me off, I saw a game cart and fresh blood in the bed of one of their pickups."

"That wouldn't surprise me any. They probably just finished carting half a beef into the garage for butchering."

"Probably, but then again, they might be up to something."

"So, what do you want to do?" Hargraves asked.

"I'm not sure. Let's think on it, and tomorrow let's . . . hold on, I'm getting another call. See you at the office."

McCain pressed a button on his phone to receive the incoming call from Sinclair.

"Hey, you're a TV star," he said. "I can't change the station without seeing your face."

"Yeah, it's one of the crappier parts of the job. And these young TV reporters around here ask the stupidest questions. Didn't they teach them anything in school?"

McCain knew that many of the reporters hired by the local TV stations were graduates of WSU's school of broadcast journalism. But he wasn't going to tell her that.

"Yakima is about the 126th largest TV market in the country," McCain said. "All the really good young reporters go to the bigger markets for higher pay. So, we get Simon Erickson. He's a nice, hardworking guy, but I don't think he's going to be the next Lester Holt."

McCain knew all of this because one of his buddies used to

be a news director for the ABC station in town. The buddy had done the news anchor thing, and then became the news director before taking a job with the County Health District as their public relations director.

"Didn't Tom Brokaw have a speech impediment?" Sinclair asked.

"I think so. I guess there's hope for Simon yet."

"Hey, I've heard from a couple other states on my request for similar missing or murdered women," Sinclair reported. "And a couple other things have popped up. I thought maybe we should get together to talk. I'd like to get your thoughts on it."

"I can come to your office anytime later this afternoon, if that works."

"Sure, let's meet at five. See ya then."

It was getting close to lunch time, so McCain decided he'd drop down the hill from Tieton and go into Naches for some chicken strips and a cold soda. Seeing all the chickens at the Johnsons must've had a subliminal effect on him, he thought. The little hamburger place in town made the best chicken strips, and when he had a craving for strips, he headed there. Then after lunch he could run up the Tieton River and make sure none of the anglers on the river had caught a bull trout. He definitely wanted to keep Andrea Parker off his back.

He had just picked up his order from the carry-out window and was sitting down at the picnic table in the grass next to the building when Jim Kingsbury pulled in. He must have seen McCain's truck sitting in the parking lot because he parked, jumped out of the truck, and came right over to where McCain was eating. He wore a bright yellow shirt reading PROCRASTINATE NOW in bold purple letters.

"Hey, Jim. Where's your partner?"

"He's at a doctor's appointment in Yakima. I wanted to let you know that I've been keeping tabs on that cowboy in the silver

Honda. I saw him around town a few times, and then he just disappeared."

"Okay," McCain said, chewing on a chicken strip. "So, what was he doing around here when you saw him?"

"He was in the grocery store buying a bunch of food. And then I saw him twice in the hardware store buying a big length of chain, some heavy-duty locks, and propane."

"Which way did he go after he left the hardware store?" McCain asked.

"West. I thought about following him, but Frank told me not to. He said you'd be ticked."

"Yeah, it's probably a good idea to steer clear of the guy. Besides, he's done nothing wrong that we know of. He's probably just fixing up a cabin or something near Rimrock. I've seen him up that way a couple of times."

"Okay, but just thought you'd like to know. Say, those chicken strips look good. I think I'll order me some."

After lunch McCain made his checks on the anglers up the Tieton. While stopped to talk to a man and his daughter fishing off the bank, he looked into the trees across the river and noticed a small gray box affixed to one of the cottonwood tree trunks. It took him a second, but then he realized he was looking at a digital trail camera. Hunters around the country had been purchasing them by the thousands and placing them on trees and fence posts and all sorts of other things to keep track of deer, elk, and other wildlife. The cameras were quiet, and the newer ones didn't even need a flash to catch the animals at night. Some even shot in video. They were triggered by movement, and most held the photos on a SIM card. The really fancy ones could be hooked up to smart phones and would transfer the photos to a computer or tablet, almost in real time. In a way, McCain thought, it was a bit unfair. Technology had slipped into the outdoor world, and hunters were using it everywhere.

On the way back to town he started thinking about the trail cameras. What if some hunter had one of those cameras up in the mountains where it might have taken a photo of the killer packing one of the dead women to be dropped? Or perhaps someone's home security cameras near the Bald Mountain turn-off or along the Wenas Road might have recorded the vehicles going by on the nights the women disappeared? It was long shot, but he would mention it to Sinclair when they met.

When he arrived at her office, Sinclair's big black Chrysler wasn't there, so he sat in his truck and did a little research on trail cameras on his phone. He was totally involved in what he was reading when there was a tap on his window. He jumped in surprise.

Agent Sinclair, standing there dressed in her FBI work attire of black slacks, white blouse, and black boots, was laughing.

"Sorry," she said. "I didn't mean to scare you. Thanks for meeting me."

"My pleasure," McCain said. "I've been thinking about this killer thing all afternoon. And I have some thoughts."

When they got into Sinclair's office, she told him the crime lab had come around and now believed the thin tire track McCain had found was from a game cart. The problem was, from what they could tell, several of the manufacturers used the same tire on all their carts. So, trying to find purchasers of one particular cart was going to be next to impossible. The crime lab people had also analyzed the boot imprints near the cart track and couldn't determine a make of boot or shoe. But based on the partial prints they believed the shoe size was 12 or 13.

Sinclair said a search of Jimenez's body and clothing for anything that might carry DNA of the killer was negative. She said that they had not yet found Jimenez's car. Not that it would do much good other than possibly giving an idea where the abduction had taken place. If they knew that, they could ask locals if they had seen anything the night before the new moon.

"We have the analysis from our profiler, some professor at Dartmouth," Sinclair said. "She believes it is a white male, age twenty-five to forty-five, who has some serious issues with women."

"Really," McCain said. "I could have told you that. That fits about every serial killer in the history of the world."

"I know," Sinclair said. "She's still baffled by the removal of the heart, but thinks it relates to unrequited love."

"I guess I should be a professor someplace," McCain said.

Sinclair went on to tell him that Colorado had come through with a couple of missing women that fit the profile—young, fit, long black hair. Both of them, she said, had just disappeared.

"They pulled a David Copperfield, is how the sheriff in Moffat County put it," she explained. "That's where the two women went missing. Both were normal people, working in good jobs, seemingly happy with life."

"Did you get the dates when they went missing?" McCain asked.

"Yes, a little over a year ago, about a month apart," Sinclair said.

"And did you put those dates to the moon phases?" McCain asked.

"No!" she said. "I didn't think about that."

She grabbed the dates off the email she had on her phone from the Colorado sheriff, and McCain brought up the moon phase chart.

"There you go. A perfect match to the new moon, for both of them," he said. "It's gotta be the same person."

"So, if we can find someone who worked and lived in that part of Colorado a year ago, we might have something," she said.

"Yep, and if he's a white guy, twenty-five to forty-five, with big feet, who hates women with black hair and is fit enough to pack a 120-pound body up a trail, boom, we got our guy."

"Don't forget, he owns a game cart," she said.

"I can name you about eleven guys off the top of my head that fit that, including Deputies Stratford and Williams," McCain said. "Well, except for the Colorado part, and the hating women with long black hair. And Williams might be a bit older than forty-five."

Sinclair said they were still running down calls from people who thought their neighbor, or brother-in-law, or boss was the killer, but so far nothing had even come close to panning out.

McCain told Sinclair about the whole game camera idea, and his thoughts on the home security cameras adjacent to the roads they thought the killer had driven on the nights of the new moon. Sinclair was aware of the trail cameras but didn't know how popular they had become. She thought it was a great idea.

"How do we get the word out to the hunting world, to ask if they might check their cameras in the areas where we know the bodies were found, to see if there is anything out there?" she asked.

"There are all kinds of hunting chat sites on the internet and hunting groups on Facebook," McCain said.

He knew that because now part of every fish and wildlife police officer's job was to watch those different sites and groups. In the past few years several poachers had been discovered because they couldn't help themselves and just had to show off their ill-gotten trophies. The problem was, in many of those photos, there were things in the background that tipped off authorities to the fact that the animal was taken out of season, or in a unit that wasn't open.

For instance, one guy McCain had run down claimed to have shot a big mule deer buck in one of the high mountain units during an early season hunt in September. McCain knew the area the unit was in was hit with an early snowstorm and there was snow on the ground for the duration of the season. Unfortunately for the poacher, the photo showed him with the deer in perfectly clear and dry country. Way in the background in the photo was a cell tower, which showed pretty much where the man had killed the deer.

"It's worth a shot," she said. "Let's get the word out. Remember the Ted Kaczynski thing?"

"That's John Krasinski," McCain said with a laugh.

CHAPTER 19

McCain and Hargraves met the next morning to discuss the little issue of the Johnson brothers. If they were continuing in the family tradition of poaching black bears, they were most likely doing so in familiar territory, at least that is what McCain figured. Hargraves suggested they first take a look up in the Ahtanum, where they had discovered LeRoy Junior over a bear bait in the spring. And, he thought it would be worth checking out the area to the west too, as some bears would have headed to higher country in the summer.

Hargraves would do some checking a couple miles due west of the Johnson's last bear baits, and McCain would check around in the area where the baits had been placed a few months earlier. The officers agreed to check in with each other at one o'clock.

Before he headed out to check on the bait sites, McCain went and picked up Jack. He figured the dog would like a little outing in the woods. After grabbing Jack, McCain drove west out of town on Ahtanum Road through orchards and small farm fields. When he hit the Tampico store he veered to the right and followed the north fork of Ahtanum Creek up into the area known as Nasty Creek. This is where the Johnsons had tried to score some bear bladders to sell on the black market, and odds were this is where they had returned.

McCain parked on an old logging two-track road on National Forest land and started walking up the trail. Jack crisscrossed ahead as McCain searched the surroundings for anything out of place. The Johnsons had used a camouflaged pop-up blind where Hargraves had nabbed LeRoy Junior during the spring, so he looked for those or the blue fifty-gallon plastic drums that were used as bait containers. McCain also looked for boot tracks in the dirt and found a few old tracks, but they could have been made weeks ago as Central Washington hadn't had any rain in almost two months.

He searched for a couple hours, up two more two-track roads, and was just about to turn around on a third when he was startled by a rifle shot nearby. He hadn't heard the sizzle of a bullet flying by and figured the shot wasn't meant for him. Still, the boom of the rifle was close enough that he decided to head that way and check it out.

McCain whistled for Jack. The dog had, at the sound of the gun, gone in search of something to retrieve. With Jack by his side he moved through the trees in the direction of the rifle fire.

As they worked over the small hogback ridge toward the shot, McCain took it slowly, watching all around him as he walked. Jack stayed dutifully by his side. After a few more quiet steps, McCain heard someone walking down below. When he finally spotted the man moving through the brush and trees, he wasn't surprised. It was none other than LeRoy Johnson Jr.

McCain decided he wasn't up for running down another member of the Johnson family, so he snuck in closer to LeRoy who was walking with purpose and not paying much attention to what else was going on.

Because Johnson was carrying a rifle, McCain pulled his pistol. When he was within twenty yards, McCain said, "Hello, LeRoy."

LeRoy turned, and as he did he brought his rifle up level with his chest.

"State police! Drop the rifle, LeRoy," McCain shouted.

When LeRoy Junior saw the pistol aimed at him, he lowered the rifle.

"Put your rifle on the ground and step back three steps," McCain ordered.

He watched Johnson put the rifle down in the grass and back up. McCain could see the young man mouthing, "one, two, three" as he took the steps back.

McCain lowered his pistol and walked toward Johnson.

"Do you have any other weapons on you?" McCain asked.

"Jest my skinnin' knife," Johnson said.

"Well, for now, maybe you better give that to me too." McCain said.

The man obliged and gave McCain a folding knife which, on closer inspection, had fairly new blood on the handle. McCain then handcuffed Johnson and frisked him, just in case the man had forgotten about a pistol in his sock or something. McCain asked LeRoy what he was shooting at. LeRoy said he had shot at a running black bear.

"Did you hit it?" McCain asked.

"Dunno," Johnson said. "I was just goin' to look when you stopped me."

"Okay, here's what we are going to do. Let's walk back to my truck, and I'll call in some help to see if we can find the bear, if it was hit. Where is your truck parked?"

"Back at our place."

"So, how'd you get out here?"

"Teddy brung me."

"And where is Teddy now?" McCain asked. All he needed was another armed Johnson running around out here in the woods.

"He's gunna pick me up on the road at dark. Unless he's got a bear down. Then I have to wait for him awhile."

"Where's Teddy hunting?"

"He's up in Cowiche. We got some baits up there."

"I see," McCain said. "And you know bear hunting is closed right now."

"Yeah, but Aaron, he's been paying us $400 for each bear bladder we git for him. And he gives us another $200 for each hide."

"This is Aaron Armitage, Teddy's friend?"

"Yeah, Teddy likes him, but he's mean to me. He even kicks the chickens when he comes to our house."

"Sounds like a nice guy."

McCain picked up Johnson's rifle, pulled out his GPS and marked a waypoint to help him look for the bear. He then tapped his hip for Jack to come, and the two men and the yellow dog headed back to the truck.

At the truck, McCain radioed for Hargraves.

"Go ahead," Hargraves answered.

"I found LeRoy Junior hunting bears," McCain reported. "I have him in custody, but we have a couple other issues. You should probably head my way as soon as you can."

"10-4," Hargraves said. "You still up the north fork?"

"I'm up Nasty Creek off the North Fork Road. You'll see my rig. I think we need a sheriff's deputy here too. Someone needs to get LeRoy transported downtown, and we have a potential wounded bear to deal with. I have Jack with me, so we can track it down if the bear is wounded. But someone also needs to be here when Teddy shows up to pick up his brother. And we need to send a deputy to try to run down this guy who is buying the bear parts. LeRoy says it's Aaron Armitage. YSO might want to connect with Kittitas County because I think he lives up there. I know he's done time at Coyote Ridge, so they may be keeping tabs on him."

"Copy that," Hargraves said. "I'll get a deputy rolling and get them to make contact with Kittitas County, and I'll be there as quickly as I can. It'll be probably thirty minutes."

While they waited, McCain asked LeRoy about their bear poaching business. The younger Johnson told McCain they started back up hunting bears three weeks ago, and so far they'd killed four. They'd killed one the day before yesterday, Johnson said, which McCain figured might account for the blood in the back of Teddy's truck.

Hargraves showed up twenty-five minutes later, followed by Deputy Garcia a few minutes after that.

"Finding more bodies?" Garcia asked McCain as he climbed out of his SUV.

McCain ignored him and said, "Can you transport Mr. Johnson here down to the county lock-up for me? Hargraves has to be here to arrest Johnson's brother when he shows up, and I need to go deal with a possible wounded bear."

Garcia agreed to take Johnson to Yakima, so McCain took his handcuffs off the man, and Garcia cuffed him with his own and put Johnson in the backseat of his rig.

"Thanks, Paul," McCain said. "I owe you lunch."

"Yeah, yeah," Garcia said. "Don't get eaten by that bear."

Garcia drove off in a cloud of dust, and Hargraves turned to McCain and said, "Since Teddy isn't due here until dark, you want me to go help you look for that bear?"

"Naw, I think Jack and I can handle it," McCain said. "Besides, I don't want to miss Teddy. I'd hate to have him come looking for his brother and you're not here to greet him."

McCain reminded Hargraves that Teddy Johnson drove a maroon Dodge Ram 4X4, but he could possibly be in LeRoy Junior's white Chevy four-wheel drive pickup too.

"And don't be surprised if the guy makes a run for it," McCain said. "He strikes me as just the type. Hopefully, Jack and I will find the bear quickly, and we can get back to assist you."

"Go do your thing," Hargraves said. "I'll be fine."

McCain checked the GPS unit and headed back toward the waypoint. It showed it was a little over a mile away. He probably could have walked right to it without the assist from a bunch of satellites overhead, but he looked at the device anyway. Before he left his truck, he grabbed the .223 rifle out of the rack and made sure it was loaded, with a round in the chamber and a full clip underneath.

As they walked, Jack cast about, looking for whatever. There were probably a million smells in the woods this time of year, and the yellow dog seemed to be taking them all in.

When they reached the place where they had cut off the younger Johnson, McCain called Jack in and kept him close as he looked for either blood or bear tracks. It took them a while, but McCain finally spotted blood on some grass. He had Jack come in to get a good whiff of the blood and the tracks in the dirt and grass.

"Go find him boy," McCain said to the dog.

Jack started immediately working the scent. When he began tracking faster, McCain would say his name and tell him to "slow down." The last thing he wanted was to have the dog rush headlong into a wounded bear. McCain continued to see dribbles of blood here and there as Jack worked the trail, but there were never any big splotches showing the animal was mortally wounded and bleeding out.

They worked along until they hit Nasty Creek, and then Jack turned and started tracking down the small stream. McCain thought that was a good sign, as most mortally wounded animals will often head to water, and they will frequently head downhill.

Unfortunately, the bear wasn't as near to death as McCain had hoped.

CHAPTER 20

Jack was doing a good job of tracking the bear. McCain had to slow him down more frequently now, which meant they were probably getting closer to the bruin. Finally, the dog followed the tracks right up to a big thicket of wild blackberries. When Jack started growling in a low rumble, McCain called him back to his side. McCain was 99.8% sure the bear was in the bramble, and the last thing he wanted was Jack in there with a wounded and pissed-off bear.

McCain knew that bears would attack if cornered, so he stood at the ready, trying to figure out what to do next. Before he'd devised his plan, he heard a "whoof" sounding like a big dog with a sore throat. McCain raised his rifle just in time to see a big black head emerge from the berry patch with a rumbling black body right behind. Not surprisingly, the bear was headed right at him. McCain heard Jack bark and saw a yellow flash headed at the bear.

Time slowed down for McCain as he calculated in microseconds how fast the bear was running and where he needed to aim to stop the bear in one shot without hitting Jack. Rather than aim, McCain instinctually pointed and pulled the trigger. All the years shooting at jackrabbits with a little .22 caliber rifle when he was a kid culminated in that moment. It was a life or death situation, for Jack, and for him. McCain squeezed the trigger and started calculating where to make the next shot.

Thankfully, he didn't have to worry about it. The beast was dead before it did a face plant in the grass just three yards in front of him.

McCain looked around for Jack. The dog was just coming into the flank of the bear, barking and dancing like a boxer, in and out, just in case the bruin came back to life.

"We're good," McCain said to Jack. "He's dead."

Although the bullet hole right between the bruin's eyes told the whole story, McCain still poked the bear a couple times to make sure he was, in fact, dead. Then he sat down and called Jack over.

"Good boy," he said to Jack as he rubbed the dog's sides and scratched his ears. "I couldn't have done that without you."

McCain marked the location of the bear on his GPS, and then he and Jack followed the creek down to where it crossed the Forest Service road. They ended up about three-quarters of a mile up the road from where McCain's truck was parked. They had just hit the road and were headed back to the truck when around the corner came Hargraves in his pickup.

"I heard the shot, and thought I might catch you up this way," Hargraves said. "So, what happened?"

"You have a good sharp knife?" McCain asked.

Hargraves said he did, in his utility box in his truck. McCain asked him to grab it and then as they hiked back up the creek to the dead bear, he told Hargraves the whole story.

"Do you need some clean shorts?" Hargraves asked. "I think I would."

Jack knew exactly where they were going and sprinted ahead to the bear.

The two men field dressed the bear, removing the innards and organs from the beast so the meat could cool, and then dragged the carcass down to Hargrave's truck. They didn't skin the bear. They would leave that to the butcher, where the bear would be taken for processing. The meat then would be donated to a food bank, or the Mission in Yakima.

As they were dragging the bear, Hargraves said, "It would sure be nice to have one of those game carts."

McCain laughed.

During a much-needed breather with a bottle of water, the two WDFW officers discussed how they might box Teddy Johnson in when he arrived. They decided Hargraves would wait behind the Tampico store, out of sight of the main road but in a spot where he could watch the North Fork Road. McCain would park about a mile past where he had found LeRoy Junior earlier and would prepare for the arrival of Teddy, once Hargraves radioed that the maroon Dodge Ram was on the way up the road. He would block the road with his truck, and Hargraves would come in from behind, so theoretically, they'd have Johnson trapped.

The sun had gone down behind the hills and light was fading when Teddy Johnson blew by the Tampico store headed to Nasty Creek. Hargraves radioed McCain, told him that Johnson was headed his way, and then pulled out, staying far enough behind that Johnson couldn't see him.

There was still enough light that Hargraves could see the dust clouds rolling up above the brush and trees as Johnson drove up the dirt road ahead of him, which helped him track the truck as well. Occasionally he would radio McCain and give him an update.

Finally, McCain radioed back and said, "I see the running lights and the dust clouds. He's getting close. Maybe move up a little closer."

"10-4," said Hargraves into the radio and pushed the Ford a bit harder.

As soon as Teddy saw the WDFW pickup in the road ahead of him he slammed on the brakes, threw it into reverse, and backed with amazing speed and control back down the road. He noticed the WDFW pickup coming up fast behind him, so he whipped the Ram into a tiny two-track side road and backed up as fast as the Dodge could go. As it turned out, it was too fast. Teddy missed a slight turn in the road, bounced over a stout rock, and the back end of the truck flew just high enough to land onto an old stump.

Johnson was high-centered, and even with the four-wheel drive trying to pull the truck off the stump from the front, he wasn't going anywhere. Teddy tried to get the truck unstuck for about three seconds, but seeing it was futile he jumped from the cab and started running.

The two officers were just pulling up next to Teddy's rig when he jumped and ran. Both were out of their trucks in an instant. McCain in front, Hargraves right behind. Hargraves saw a yellow flash take off out of McCain's truck and knew Jack was on the chase too.

"Stop, Teddy!" McCain yelled as he ran behind the man, but it was of no use.

McCain almost laughed as he thought about chasing down another Johnson. He'd just told himself only a few hours earlier he didn't want to have to do this again.

Teddy kept running and might still be running if Jack hadn't come up on him and clipped his right heel from behind. Johnson tripped and went down rolling, like a short, round human bowling ball. It was most likely an accident that Jack had hit the man's leg as it was coming back, but it sure did the job of putting him down.

McCain got to Teddy first, and even though he had the

guy by almost ten inches and twenty pounds, Johnson wasn't intimidated. He was built like a fire hydrant and was tough. He took a swing and hit McCain in the shoulder. Johnson wound up to swing again when he stiffened, started shaking and fell over.

McCain looked at Hargraves, who was holding his Taser. He'd just hit Teddy with five seconds of 50,000 volts. It didn't matter how strong the man was, he definitely was feeling the effects of the electricity. It was known technically as "electrical pulse incapacitation." And incapacitate it did.

"You can thank me later," Hargraves said with a smile on his face.

"Hey, I had him just where I wanted him," McCain said. "But I'll go ahead and thank you now."

McCain put his handcuffs on his second Johnson of the day, and he helped the dazed man to his feet.

"That was quite a move Jack put on him," Hargraves said. "Did you train him to do that?"

"Nope, that was all Jack," McCain said. "I'm glad he did it though. I wasn't gaining much ground on Teddy here. Those short little legs of his were churning pretty fast."

"Screw you," Teddy said. "Where's my brother?"

"I'm guessing by now he's in a cell right next to your father," Hargraves said. "And they're saving a spot for you too. It will be like one big family reunion."

When they got Johnson secured in the backseat of Hargraves' truck, the two officers went and looked through the Dodge. There were no bear parts, but as McCain had seen before, there were signs of dried blood in the bed of the truck. They found a rifle and a shotgun under the bench seat in the front of the truck and confiscated them.

Hargraves took Johnson to Yakima to be booked into the county jail, while McCain awaited the wrecker that would be arriving, whenever the spirit moved them, to pull Teddy's truck off the stump and haul it to the impoundment yard next to the sheriff's office.

McCain told himself he'd wait for an hour to meet the wrecker and show them where the truck was. If they didn't show up by then, they could just find the thing by themselves. He knew Jack was starving, as it was way past his dinner time, and McCain was feeling a little peckish himself.

The next day, with a search warrant in hand, Hargraves, McCain, and Jack went up to the Johnson place in Tieton to look for more bear parts and anything else that might incriminate the two men in their quest for bear bladders. This time they found no buried bear parts. They did, however, find a couple plastic containers in a refrigerator out in the garage with a bladder in each.

The day after the Johnson brothers had been arrested, Kittitas County sheriff's deputies located and arrested Aaron Armitage. He was staying at Teddy's cabin in Cle Elum. They had a search warrant, based on the arrest of Teddy, and found two more plastic containers with bladders in them, along with four bear hides rolled up in plastic bags in a chest freezer.

CHAPTER 21

One evening, a few days after the run-in with the Johnson brothers, McCain was at home, replenishing his to-go pack with more snacks and water when he started thinking about the little toothpick wrapper he had picked up in the mountains and given to Sinclair. He again wondered if it might have come from the vehicle the killer used to transport the body. He and Sinclair had really spent very little time in Antonio's the night they went, so he decided to visit the bar again. It was a longshot, but he decided to check it out.

He left Jack in the cool air-conditioned house, jumped into his Tundra and headed to Yakima. McCain wasn't sure what or who he expected to find when he arrived at the place, but figured he'd go into the bar, look around, and have a chat with the bartender. It took him a while, but he found a place to park and headed for the bar. As he entered, he was almost overwhelmed by the number of people in the place. It might have been busier and louder than when he was there with Sinclair. The tables were all full, as were all the seats at the bar. Once his eyes adjusted from the bright evening light outside, McCain scanned the room and caught the eyes of a familiar face looking right back at him.

"Crap," he said to himself. It was Andrea Parker. As soon as she saw him, she headed his way. The biologist from work didn't look like a biologist now. Most of the time she wore glasses, and her hair was usually up in a bun. But tonight there were no spectacles, and her light brown hair was down over her shoulders. McCain tried not to look, but there was plenty of cleavage bursting out of her low-cut red top too.

"Hey, Luke," Parker said. "I don't think I've seen you in here before."

"Well, you know me," he said. "I'm not a big drinker."

"So, what brings you here tonight?" she asked.

"I'm looking for a buddy," he said. "But I don't see him."

"Do I know him?" she asked.

"I don't think so," McCain said. "He's here once in a while. I was driving by and thought I would just stick my head in to see if he's here tonight and say hello."

"Why didn't you call him?" she asked.

McCain wanted to say, "It's none of your damn business!" but instead he said, "I did, no answer. I figured he might not be able to hear his phone as loud as this place is."

"You can come join us if you want," she said.

"Aw, I better not," McCain said. "My dog's at home and if I don't make it back fairly soon, he'll get mad at me and pee on the couch or something."

Parker made a face like she'd just smelled a fart and said, "Well, just thought I would ask. See you at work."

"Not if I see you first," he said, quiet enough that she couldn't hear him over the roar of the bar crowd as she walked away.

Before he turned and walked out, he took another hard look around the bar and saw no one else he recognized. He walked over to the bar, and when the bartender came over, McCain said, "I'm looking for a friend. About my age, well-built guy, dark brown hair, a little shorter than me, wears a cowboy hat sometimes."

The bartender thought about it a few seconds and said, "Sounds like about half the dudes who come in here, except for the cowboy hat. This isn't a goat-roper bar. I don't think I've ever seen anyone with a cowboy hat in here."

"Yeah, okay, well thanks," McCain said as he turned and headed for the door. When he stepped through the threshold, he ran headlong into Deputies Williams, Stratford and Garcia. In fact, he about bowled them over.

"Hey, slow down," Garcia said, kind of pissed. Then he saw who it was. "Oh hey, McCain."

McCain stopped and looked at the three guys, all off duty in street clothes, and said, "Hey, guys."

"What's the big hurry?" Williams asked.

"Jack's at the neighbors, and I need to take him off their hands before he eats them outta house and home," he lied.

"No time to join us for dinner?" Garcia asked. "I remember something about you owing me one for hauling that bear poacher into town for you the other day."

"I believe I said lunch," McCain said. "Besides, this place is way too rich for my blood. I was thinking more along the lines of Miner's, or for you, McDonald's."

"Stratford here is the big spender," Williams said. "He's celebrating his one-year anniversary with the department, and he's buying."

"Food's good here?" McCain asked Stratford.

"So, I've heard," he said. "I've never eaten here before."

Everyone said quick goodbyes, and the three deputies went on into the bar as McCain headed to his truck.

As he drove home, McCain thought about running into the deputies. He wondered if it really was Stratford's first time dining there. What about Williams and Garcia? He wondered how often they stopped in for a drink.

Sinclair called him first thing the next morning. McCain was just loading Jack into the truck to head up Chinook Pass to Bumping Lake. A woman had called in and said she thought she had shot a cougar that had been prowling around the cabins. Evidently one of the neighbor's cock-a-poos was missing, and they were worried the mountain lion might have taken up snacking on family pets. The woman who called in said she saw the cougar sneaking up on another neighbor's dog, so she pulled out her husband's 30-30 rifle and shot at the cat.

"Hey!" McCain said into the phone. "I think Simon the TV reporter has a little crush on you. I've seen you on TV with him like four times now."

"Yeah, yeah," she said. "Listen, we might have something on your idea about the trail cameras. We got a call from a local guy who just reviewed his photos from April and thinks there's something on one of his cameras we might want to see."

"When can you see them?"

"I told the guy we'd come by later today. Are you available at four?"

McCain told her he was, and she gave him the address for SPD&G Accounting on the west side of Yakima. McCain told her he'd meet her at the accounting company at four o'clock and clicked off.

As he drove up toward Chinook Pass and Bumping Lake, McCain wondered what might be on the trail cameras. Even if it was a photo of a person, possibly the killer, would they be able to see enough detail in the dark of the new moon night to tell who it was?

When he arrived at the little resort on Bumping Lake, a petite, silver-haired lady of about seventy-five, wearing tan shorts, a pink hooded sweatshirt and a pink tennis visor, came hustling out of the store.

"Mrs. Thomas?" McCain asked as he climbed out of his WDFW pickup. "I'm Luke McCain."

"Yes, I'm Hilda Thomas," the lady said. "I assume you know why I called?"

"I do. Can you take me to where you shot at the cougar?"

"I can," she said. "I would never think of shooting such a beautiful animal, but the thing was stalking the Olson's dog, Duke. And you heard that a cougar snatched the Puttman's little cock-a-poo?"

"I did," McCain said. "Should we drive, or can we walk?"

"We can walk. That way you can see the cougar tracks."

McCain opened the door, let Jack out, and started out after the little lady who was moving up the road at a brisk pace. When they caught up to her, she turned and looked at Jack. "That's a beautiful Lab. Aren't they the best? Bob and I have had six Labs over the years, and they've all been really good pets. And they were good hunters too. Bob used to hunt pheasants and ducks, and our Labs went everywhere with him."

"They are great hunters and pets," McCain agreed. "Jack here, he's mostly a chow hound. But once in a while he earns his keep."

Jack was looking around to see if there were any squirrels that needed chasing.

"Right here is one of the cougar tracks," Thomas said, pointing to the dirt road. "See it. The thing's been prowling around here for days."

Sure enough, there in the middle of the road, just as plain as day, was a mountain lion track. And by the size of the track, it was a big cat.

"Has anyone actually seen the cougar?"

"We've only caught glimpses of it in the headlights driving in and out of here at night. Well, that is, until I saw it today ready to pounce on Duke."

"Any other pets missing besides the cock-a-poo?"

"No, but after Sheryl's little LuLu went missing, everyone has kept their dogs close by."

"Good plan. Now where did you shoot at the cougar?"

Mrs. Thomas led him past three more cabins and then turned to go around the back of the fourth.

"This is our cabin here," she said as she walked quickly toward the back. "I was finishing up some dishes and looked out the window and saw Duke over by those trees. He likes to chase the squirrels. Then I saw a slight movement past the trees, and when I looked closer I could see it was a cougar, and he was staring right at the dog."

The woman told McCain that her husband had passed away the year before, but he had taught her how to shoot, and she always kept a loaded rifle in the closet for protection.

"I've shot a couple coyotes that were slinking around here," she said. "But never a cougar."

McCain had her walk him over to where she thought the mountain lion was when she last saw it. Then he asked her to go back to her cabin.

"I'm going to go back to my truck and bring it up here. Then Jack and I will see if you hit the cougar, and if we can find it."

"Oh, I hit it," Thomas said. "I rarely miss."

When McCain got back to where the cougar was last seen, he was carrying his shotgun. He figured buck shot at close range would be a better option if they were dealing with a wounded cougar. He searched the ground for a bit, keeping Jack at heel, and found the cougar's tracks. He followed them for a few yards and then he saw blood. Sure enough, the confident little lady had not missed. Now, he hoped she had delivered a fatal shot.

McCain put Jack on the track and let him go, knowing that cougars will almost always climb a tree if pursued. But he didn't need to worry about it. The dog only had gone about 200 yards when he found the cat, dead in a puddle of blood.

"I guess this old tom cat has eaten his last cock-a-poo," McCain said to Jack. "Good job!"

As McCain dragged the dead cat back to his truck, he was trying to decide whether he needed to issue any kind of ticket to the nice little Hilda Thomas. He certainly could make a case that she had shot the cat out of season, without a license or tag. On the other hand, she was protecting personal property, even if it wasn't hers.

Back at the truck he lifted the cougar up to his tailgate and examined it a little closer. The cat was very skinny, and his teeth were worn down to about nothing. No wonder he had turned to poaching pets, McCain thought. His days were numbered.

Based on that, he decided to not bother Mrs. Thomas with any tickets or fines. He went back, knocked on her door and told her that Jack had found the cougar, dead from a 30-30 bullet.

"I knew I hit it," the little lady said. "I rarely miss."

"Well, even though you got this one, it would probably be best if you call us if you see another cougar around the cabins. And, tell the folks around here to keep their pets close," McCain instructed as he handed her his card.

As he was driving back toward town, McCain tried to envision Mrs. Thomas shooting the cougar. He was pretty impressed.

Soon after, McCain met Sinclair at the offices of Jeffry Smith, one of the owners of the accounting firm. Smith, a slim man of about five foot, ten inches, looked like a runner, or a bike rider. McCain couldn't tell which. He was one of those guys that McCain always felt like offering a hoagie sandwich and a big piece of chocolate cake. With a thin face, and sunken cheeks, the man looked to be in a perpetual state of hunger.

"I saw your post on the Washington Bowhunter's site," Smith said. "I use the trail cameras for scouting purposes and just finally had the chance to go through the photos. I like to keep the cameras up all year just to see what's out there. I've had a few stolen over the years, but most of the time if you place them right, you won't lose them. And I've gotten some amazing photos."

Smith explained that as an accountant he was extremely busy during March and April, filing taxes for businesses and people, so he hadn't had a chance to check his cameras. And then, he had injured an Achilles tendon during a 5K mountain run up by Clear Lake, so he was on crutches for three months. He was only just now finally fit enough to get up to his cameras and check them out.

When he pulled up the photos that he thought Sinclair might be interested in, McCain could see nothing but a dark screen at first. Then McCain looked closer, and he saw the outline of what appeared to be a moth.

"I saw the moth," Smith said. "I thought, nothing to see here, and I was just about to delete the photo when that darker spot in the upper right corner caught my eye."

McCain and Sinclair moved in closer to look at the image on the computer screen. Smith scrolled over and enlarged the dark spot. It was grainy and very blurry, but it was definitely the image of a man, and he was pushing a game cart.

The date stamp on the photo was March 9, the day after Sonya Alverez had gone missing. Smith told McCain the camera was just off the road up Milk Canyon, above the Wenas.

"Can you pinpoint exactly on the map where this camera was?" McCain asked.

"I can do one better," Smith said. "I have that onX map program, and I mark every one of my cameras, just so I can find them quickly."

The accountant pulled out his smart phone, opened the map, and zoomed into where the camera in question was placed.

McCain was interested to see why the camera had caught the killer but didn't have any photos of investigators or the recovery team.

"We parked about 300 yards up the road from there," McCain explained. "Did you get any other people on that camera?"

"Actually, I do have a few other photos with people and dogs in them," Smith said. "Here's one with a young guy and gal. And another with a golden retriever."

"Those are the kids who found the body when they were shed hunting," McCain said. "And that was their dog, Mutt, or maybe it was Jeff."

Sinclair and McCain stared at the photo of the man and the cart, but with so little detail, there was no real way to identify him. McCain looked at the man's head for a cowboy hat. That certainly would have been recognizable, but he could see nothing.

"I'll send the photo to our lab and let the technicians play with it," Sinclair said. "But frankly, I'm guessing they're not going to be able to do much with it."

Sinclair gave her email address to Smith, so he could send the trail camera photo to her. She and McCain thanked Smith for calling and helping with the investigation.

"I'm guessing you're right," McCain said as they walked back to their rigs. "It's something but it's probably not going to help much."

"All we can do is keep thinking and checking stuff out," she said. "Sooner or later we'll get a break."

"Sooner would be good with me," McCain said.

"Me too," she agreed.

CHAPTER 22

The hot summer days of August quickly turned into the hot summer days of early September. Nothing was shaking on the investigation of the Cascade Killer. Sinclair was getting frustrated, and McCain felt that if they didn't do something soon, they might have another dead woman out there somewhere.

McCain had been thinking about the other women who had done the David Copperfield in Colorado, and he decided he'd like to chat with the sheriff of Moffat County. He was just finishing up some computer work before heading home to feed Jack and decided to give the sheriff a call.

He forgot that Colorado was an hour ahead of Washington, so when he called he got a dispatcher who said Sheriff Armstrong was off duty. McCain gave the dispatcher his cell number and asked her to have the sheriff give him a call any time.

Surprisingly, Sheriff Armstrong called him back about ten minutes later.

"Hello, this is McCain," he said into his phone.

"Yeah, this is Bill Armstrong down here in Craig, Colorado," the sheriff said. "What can I do you for?"

"I've been sort of involved in this serial killer investigation here in Washington," McCain said. "I think you talked to the FBI about the possible connection between our four dead women and a couple of missing women down your way?"

"Yessir," Armstrong said. "It sounds like pretty similar circumstances. By the way, how can you be sort of involved? Isn't that like being sort of pregnant?"

McCain explained that he wasn't officially on the task force that was doing the investigation, but he and his yellow Lab Jack had been involved in locating two of the women's bodies and he had figured out the whole deal about the new moon.

Armstrong hadn't been told about the new moon aspect, and when McCain explained it to him, the sheriff said, "Okay, you've got my attention now."

"Well, I actually have three names of people I'd like to have you check in your database if possible," McCain said. "I'm just looking to see if they had a Colorado driver's license and an address somewhere in your neck of the woods during the time those two women went missing."

"I can do that," Armstrong said. "We're a pretty small department here in Moffat County, but I can get the state police to run them for me. Shoot me the names."

"I'll do you one better," McCain said. "I'll send you Washington driver's licenses on all three. Give me your email address and I'll send them as soon as I have them in hand."

McCain already had the license for the cowboy, Chad Burke, but he could get the other two with one quick phone call, which is exactly what he did. When he had all three, he sent them to Sheriff Armstrong with a note that simply said, "*Thanks!*"

The response from Moffat County was waiting for him when arrived in the office the next morning. They had three matches on different Chad Burkes, but only one, based on the photo on the Colorado driver's license, was an actual match. He'd lived in the small ski resort town of Steamboat Springs, just east of Moffat County. McCain looked up a map of Colorado on the internet and figured Steamboat Springs was within easy driving distance of Craig.

The other two names McCain had given the sheriff came up with name matches but no exact matches based on the photos in the driver's licenses. McCain thought about it for a few seconds. After looking at the Colorado map again, he had one more idea he thought might be worth checking out. He emailed Sheriff Armstrong to see if he could do it for him. The sheriff emailed back a few minutes later. He said it might take a day or so, but he'd check.

With that, McCain headed out into the early September heat to go do what he was paid to do. As hot as it was, he decided he'd head to the mountains and check some of the anglers up at Leech Lake, Dog Lake, and Clear Lake near White Pass. It would definitely be cooler up there. He envied Jack. He'd left him in the air-conditioned house. The big yellow dog was probably sprawled out sleeping on McCain's bed at that very moment.

On his way up Highway 12, McCain thought about the woman he had seen with the cowboy that night on the sidewalk. He sure wished he had seen her face. And he hoped she was living a happy life wherever she was at this moment.

When McCain hit Rimrock Lake he slowed a bit as he drove by. There were a few boats out on the lake, but from what he could see they were all pulling skiers or tubers.

As he neared Indian Creek Corrals, McCain saw Ray Patterson out at the rails of one of the corrals, so he swung in for a minute. He rolled down the passenger window and Patterson walked over. Patterson was thin, about six feet tall, and wore cowboy boots and a t-shirt tucked into tight Wranglers. He had a little hitch in his giddy-up, most likely from his younger days team roping in the pro rodeo circuits.

"Hi, Luke," Patterson said. "How's the search for that serial killer going?"

"Kinda slow," McCain said. "But I'm not too involved. Say, did you ever get paid for letting everyone use your horses that day those bones were found up the Twin Sisters trail?"

"Yep, paid in full," Patterson said. "From the county too, which is a switch. Usually I'm sending them money."

"That's the truth," McCain said.

The two men chewed the fat for a few more minutes. McCain asked how business had been, and Patterson said it had been a good summer so far.

"Lots of people are renting horses and going up and looking at the spot where the bones were found," Patterson said. "That's pretty creepy if you ask me, but hey, they're renting my ponies, so I'm okay with it I guess."

McCain said so long to Patterson and headed on up the highway, toward Dog Lake to check the anglers there.

On his way home he saw the silver Honda sitting in front of the grocery store in Naches. McCain now knew that Burke had lived in Colorado, not far from where the women went missing. He decided to stop in and chat with the cowboy again.

Just as he was pulling into the store's parking lot, Burke was coming out with an armload of groceries.

McCain pulled up next to the Honda and got out.

"Hey, how's the rafting going?"

"Good. Lots of people right now, what with the weather being so nice. The offer still stands if you'd like to try it."

"You know what, I would. Would you have room for a friend of mine too?"

"I think we can make that happen. I can take you tomorrow or Sunday. Just give me a call."

"Let me get your number, I'll check with my friend, and we'll get it all set up. I remember you saying you moved up here from Colorado. Did you whitewater guide down there as well?"

"No, I was basically a ski bum. I taught some ski lessons and did a little guiding on the streams in Northern Colorado. But it didn't pay the bills, so I came up here where the grass was greener."

"I'm envious," McCain said.

"Yeah, well, let me know about the raft trip," Burke said and climbed into the Honda and fired it up.

McCain watched him drive off and then called Sinclair.

"Hey, McCain. What's up?" she said when she answered.

"What you got going tomorrow or Sunday?"

"Just gotta keep pushing on this case, why?"

"I think you need a break. I've set up a whitewater rafting trip for you and me. We just need to pick the day."

"I guess I can make tomorrow work."

"Okay, let me get the details, and I'll text you a time. Maybe you can meet me at my house, and we'll go from there."

"Sounds great, thanks."

McCain called Burke to get the meeting time and place. The float down the Tieton River only took about three hours, so they ran them in the afternoon on most days, according to Burke. He told McCain to meet the raft company bus at the Windy Point campground at noon. "And wear clothes you don't mind getting wet," the cowboy said. "See you tomorrow."

McCain texted Sinclair to meet at his house at 11:15 and told her about the clothing suggestion. She arrived promptly at 11:15, dressed in gray shorts, a green Oregon Ducks t-shirt under an unbuttoned denim shirt, and a San Francisco 49'ers ball cap on.

"This should be fun. What made you think of it?"

"It will be fun," McCain said. "But I have some ulterior motives."

McCain went on to tell her his history with Chad Burke and about seeing the silver Honda up in the mountains not far from where one of the bodies was found back in the spring. And he told her about seeing Burke with a woman with long black hair in Naches. And most importantly, he told her about Burke's past in Colorado, living near where the women went missing at the time they disappeared.

"I know it's all circumstantial, but I thought you'd like to meet the guy."

"Definitely," she said. "If nothing else, the rafting trip should be fun."

"Wait one minute. I gotta grab one more thing, and then we can be on our way."

"Where's Jack?" Sinclair asked.

"He's over at the neighbors being spoiled rotten."

McCain ran into the house, and three minutes later he came out wearing a crimson and gray WSU t-shirt and black ball cap with a big WSU logo on it.

"Hey, you're flying the colors, so will I."

Sinclair just shook her head and laughed.

When they got to the campground, they found three big blue buses sitting there along with about forty people meandering around. The guides were obvious because they were already outfitted in blue personal floatation vests and helmets.

"That's our guy, right there next to the back of the second bus," McCain said.

Sinclair laughed again. "I know that guy. I see him working out sometimes in the evenings at my gym. He's even asked me out."

"Well, isn't that special," McCain said sarcastically. "Here I think I've found a possible suspect and you're doing Zumba with him."

"Doesn't mean he's not a suspect," she said. "Especially knowing what we know now. Let's go enjoy the day and see where it leads."

"10-4," McCain said as he opened the truck door and headed to the rafts and Burke.

The cowboy recognized Sinclair immediately and said, "Hey, nice to see you out here. Glad the game warden brought you along. You ready for some fun?"

"Sure am," Sinclair said. "I guess I never asked you what you did for a living when we talked at the gym. This is a cool job."

"It's fun, you meet lots of great people, and I'm outdoors, where I want to be. But the pay's not great."

"Well, it definitely beats sitting behind a desk staring at a computer all day."

"If you guys are ready, let's load up."

McCain and Sinclair headed to the bus. Burke just stood and stared at Sinclair and smiled.

CHAPTER 23

The heat was insufferable. The killer was burning up. He had to do something. He was having the nightmares again. He had to make them stop.

She was beautiful in his dreams. Tall, pretty, with long black hair. He could still remember exactly how she looked the last time he saw her. Before she left him with those terrible people. He was only five years old, but he remembered that day like it was yesterday. As he would for the rest of his life.

She broke his heart. Tore it out really, is what she did. How could his mother, someone he had loved so much, the person who was supposed to protect him and love him, do that to him? He couldn't understand it.

He'd gotten revenge for the beatings. The man and the woman, who his mother said were relatives, got what was coming to them. How could he be related to such horrible people? He would never believe that.

He'd only been fifteen at the time, when he did what he had to do.

After they had passed out from another night of drinking, he zip-tied their wrists and ankles and shoved dirty underwear and socks in their mouths. Then he waited until they woke up. He still remembers looking into their eyes when they saw what he was doing. They squirmed and made plenty of sounds, but the filthy gags kept them muffled. They could do nothing but watch.

He turned on the gas to the stove but didn't light it. The gas slowly seeped into the old, rundown house until it hit the candle he had lit in the old utility room where they made him sleep. He was a quarter mile away when the house exploded. He thought about the two people who were inside. He hoped they were awake to feel the heat. And to feel their bodies burning. It would be like that for them for the rest of eternity, because if there was anybody who deserved to burn in hell, it was them.

He stood in the black of night, the darkest night of the month, and watched the flames. It was the night of the new moon. The perfect night to watch the house burn to the ground.

No firetrucks came. No police came. No neighbors came. No one seemed to notice the house, and the horrible people who lived inside were gone. No one cared. He'd done the world a favor.

And on that night he promised himself that he would find his mother. And he would make her pay for what she had done to him. He would make her feel the pain. He would make her know what it is like to have your heart ripped from your chest.

The heat was rising. A new moon was coming. He had to do something. He had to make the nightmares stop.

I t was three days before the new moon. McCain made a mental note of the date, and as the day drew closer his concern grew about what the killer might do next. From the past abductions and killings, the killer had taken the women the day before the new moon, seemingly at night, killed them by strangulation at some point in the next twenty-four hours, and then dumped them on the night of the new moon.

McCain believed the killer would most likely grab the woman on Friday night, the night before the next new moon. McCain and Sinclair had discussed the possibility that if the killer were to strike again, it could happen that night.

"Just for the heck of it, I'm going to keep an eye on Burke," she said.

"Good idea," McCain said. "Jack and I are going to my neighbor kid's football game."

McCain had been down at the county courthouse as a possible witness in an illegal fish-selling case, but just before the trial was to start, the attorneys struck a deal. That was just fine with him. With no trial he headed to his office. When he got there, he turned on his computer and checked his emails. First up was a reply from the sheriff in Colorado. It turned out McCain's hunch had been right. One of the other men on his list had had a job in Green River, Wyoming, in Sweetwater County, just across the state line from Moffat County, Colorado.

So that's two, McCain thought to himself.

He hadn't been surprised that the third name on his list hadn't showed up, but he wanted to check it out just so he could eliminate him as a suspect. He knew he was stretching on all of them, frankly, but with two having been within fairly close driving distance of where the women in Colorado had disappeared, and when they had disappeared, it made them that much more interesting.

Sinclair had seen Burke a couple of times at the gym after the river rafting trip. They chatted some, and since Sinclair wanted to watch him she decided the best way would be to ask him to dinner for Friday night.

"Aren't you and the game warden a thing?" he asked.

"No," she said. "We're just friends. So, what do you think?"

"Yeah, I'd be up for it. Just let me know when and where."

They decided to meet at the Thai King Restaurant, located

a couple of blocks off Yakima Avenue. Sinclair liked Thai and as it turned out so did Burke.

They met there at seven. Once they got their table and ordered, Burke asked, "So what do you do for work?"

"I work in the federal court," Sinclair said. It was a lie, of course, but just a little one, because she often spent her days at the federal courthouse. When she told him, you could see his eyes glaze over just a little.

"You must really enjoy your outdoor jobs," she said, turning the subject back to him. It was a good move, because he talked for a half hour straight on his love of fishing and skiing and water rafting.

They sat and ate and talked for what seemed to Sinclair to be hours. Finally, when she'd had enough, she looked at her phone, saw it was past nine and said, "I really need to be going. I have a couple of important meetings in the morning."

"Really? Working on Saturday?" Burke asked. "Doesn't sound like government work to me. Don't you guys take off for Arbor Day and stuff like that?"

"Yeah, well, tomorrow isn't one of those days," she said.

They walked together out to their cars. They said their good nights, and she jumped into her big black Chrysler. Burke watched her drive off and then hopped into his silver Honda, started it up and turned out of the parking lot, going the other direction.

McCain decided to play a hunch. He'd told Sinclair he was going to Austin Meyer's football game, but the kid's team didn't play at night. So, with nothing better to do, and since it was the night before the new moon, he took a chance. He loaded

Jack into his Tundra and, with an address he had from a driver's license, headed east toward Terrace Heights.

After following the road out past the landfill, McCain found a spot in a small orchard and parked far enough away from the rundown double wide to not cause suspicion, but close enough to where he could watch the place with his binoculars. It wasn't quite dark, but there were no cars in the driveway and there were no lights on inside the manufactured home. From what he could tell no one was home.

"We'll just wait here for a while and see what transpires," McCain said to Jack.

The yellow dog wagged his tail and curled up on the passenger seat.

CHAPTER 24

The killer was waiting for her behind some arborvitae next to her house. As she pulled her car in under the carport he snuck around the back of the car. He watched, and as soon as she was stepping up out of the car, he hit her, hard, in the back of the head with his fist. Unlike some of the other women, she didn't go down, but it stunned her. He hit her again, and this time she went to her knees.

He quickly pulled the zip ties out of his pocket, secured her wrists and ankles, opened the back door of her car and pushed her in. He stuffed a rag in her mouth, and to keep her lying down in the back seat, he buckled the seat belt around her and pulled it tight. Then he dug through her purse, found her keys, jumped into the driver's seat, started the engine, backed out and took off.

It had all taken about thirty seconds. As he drove away, he looked around to make sure no one had seen him or was following them.

On the drive to his house he kept an eye on the rearview mirror. No one was following him. With the other women he had taken them in his car. For the sake of time, he decided to use her car. His vehicle would be fine where he parked it.

He drove out Terrace Heights Drive, past the Chevy dealership and Walmart, and out beyond the cemetery and the grade school. He was just past the landfill when she started squirming in the backseat. He looked back at her a couple times as he drove, and he was looking back when they went by the little orchard where McCain was parked in the trees, back off the road.

McCain saw the big black car roll by, and even though there were a few others like that around, he was pretty sure it was Sinclair's. What he couldn't quite figure out was, what she was doing out here right now. If she had the same hunch he had, wouldn't she be bringing some back-up? He decided to just sit and watch. The problem was it was dark, and with very little moon and hardly any lights around the house, it was hard to see exactly what was going on.

Through his binoculars McCain saw the black car pull up close to the front door of the double wide and saw the driver's door open. He couldn't tell exactly who got out, but he knew it wasn't Sinclair. It was a man.

The guy went to the front door of the house, opened it and came back to the car. He opened the passenger door on the driver's side, lifted a woman out of the car and carried her in.

McCain couldn't tell who the woman was, nor could he tell if she was passed out or dead. She definitely wasn't putting up a fight. Because it looked like Sinclair's car, he had to assume it was her.

"We gotta get up there, Jack," he said. The dog's ears perked up at the sound of his name. A second later he was standing in his seat.

Before they headed toward the house, McCain called 911 and gave them his location. Then he grabbed his service pistol in his holster and attached it to his belt. He also put his Taser in his pocket, and then he and Jack jumped out of the truck. They worked quickly through the orchard, then up the hill to the house.

The killer placed her in the same chair where he had put the others. He zip-tied her ankles to the legs of the chair and secured her wrists behind her around the back of the chair.

When he looked at her he realized she was different. Yes, she was fit and pretty and had long black hair, but when he looked in her eyes he didn't see the fear that he had seen in the other women's eyes. All he saw in her eyes was rage. She was flat out mad, which scared him for a second.

He double checked the plastic ties and then he got in front of her. He explained to her that he really didn't want to do all of this, but he had to punish her. He had to hurt her like she had hurt him. He asked her why she had left him with the horrible people. Why had she abandoned him with the people who beat him and treated him worse than their dogs? He asked her why she never returned to get him, to save him.

The more he talked to the woman the madder he got. The heat was rising within him again. His voice got louder and louder and soon he was screaming at her.

McCain could hear the man talking but he couldn't see what was going on, so he slowly worked his way around the other side of the house, Jack moving quietly by his side.

He looked into one of the windows but could see nothing. The only light on in the house was in the front room, and McCain was on the other side of the house. He had to move around to get a better look.

He and Jack started moving slowly around, but McCain stopped when he heard the man's voice getting louder. He still hadn't heard Sinclair's voice, so he still didn't know if she was conscious or if she was gagged.

They continued moving around the house, stopping to listen when the man's voice was raised, in obvious anger. Finally, McCain noticed a crack in the blinds and peeked through. He could see the back of the man who was again screaming in anger at Sinclair in the chair. He looked unarmed, but McCain knew he most likely had a gun nearby. The man, dressed all in black, stepped to the side just enough for McCain to get a good view of Sinclair. She was awake but gagged. Blood dripped from her head.

"Ah, shit," he said under his breath. About then he could hear sirens in the distance. Come on, get here, he thought.

He looked again and saw the man turn as he heard the sirens wail. McCain could also see the anger in Sinclair's eyes. She was tied to the chair, but he could see in her eyes she wasn't afraid.

McCain drew his pistol as the man came toward the window. "Give it up, Stratford!" McCain said. "I have cops on the way. Let's end this. I've told them who you are, and they'll be here shortly. Let Agent Sinclair go and end this now."

McCain had backed away from the window, so he had no idea what was happening in there. But he knew if the deputy was getting a gun, Sinclair was in real danger. He decided to head for the door. If he could distract Stratford enough, he could possibly get in there to save her.

He thought he had heard sirens outside. But the voices in his head were drowning them out. He loved his mother but he had to punish her for what she did. He had to punish her and then rip her heart out, like she had done to him all those years ago. As hard as he tried, he would never understand how she could do that to him when he loved her so much.

The next voice he heard wasn't in his head. It was a man's voice and it said, "Give it up, Stratford." He knew that voice. It was the damned game warden, McCain!

The cops were surely on the way, but he had played out this scenario in his head many times. He knew what he had to do. And he had to do it fast.

McCain, with Jack still by his side, stayed low and moved toward the front door. He could hear some rustling in the house but couldn't tell what was going on. When he got to the front door, McCain reached up and tried turning the doorknob. It was locked.

He listened some more and heard movement, but it was farther away. McCain decided he couldn't wait any longer. He stood up, stepped back, and with all the considerable strength he had in his 227-pound body, he kicked the door. To his surprise the door exploded open, pieces of the wood frame going everywhere. His momentum was carrying him forward, so he went with it and rolled onto the floor, coming up with his pistol ready for fire.

Sinclair was still there, zip-tied to the chair. She was moving her head in a motion that was telling him that Stratford was in the back. McCain stayed in a squatted position with his pistol pointed to the rear of the house and side-stepped slowly to Sinclair. He reached up and pulled the gag out of her mouth.

"He's gone into one of those back rooms," Sinclair whispered. Then she asked, "How did you know?"

McCain put his finger to his lips. He was listening to make sure that Stratford wasn't coming back with a shotgun or something.

Then they both heard the motorcycle. It revved once, twice, and then it was on the move.

"Damn it," McCain said. "He's running."

McCain took off toward the back of the house, Jack running right behind him. But they were too late. When he got to the back door and looked out toward the fading sound of the motorcycle, all he could see was a yellow headlight and a red taillight bouncing out through the sage brush, headed west.

CHAPTER 25

As soon as he saw Stratford getting away on the motorcycle McCain called 911, again. He told them Stratford was the killer, and that he was on the run on a motorcycle. Unfortunately, he couldn't tell the dispatcher what road the killer would end up on or what kind of a bike he was on.

McCain was cutting the restraints off Sinclair when the first sheriff's deputy arrived. It was Williams.

"What in the hell is going on?" he asked.

McCain quickly told him what had happened, and Williams got on the radio and called out an APB on Stratford, riding a motorcycle, heading west toward Yakima.

McCain continued to look after Sinclair as another sheriff's deputy and a state patrol officer joined them. A couple minutes later, an ambulance arrived.

"I don't need an ambulance," Sinclair said. "I need to get after that asshole."

"You need to be checked out," McCain said. "You said he hit you in the head hard, twice. You might have a concussion, or worse."

"I'm fine," she said. Jack had come over and was sitting at her side. She rubbed his ears.

"Stratford, who would have known?" Williams asked himself. "How did you know, McCain?"

"I didn't," he said. "Not for sure. I had an inkling, but really didn't know. I played a hunch that if it was him, he'd bring a woman here tonight. Little did I know it would be Sara."

"Boy, am I glad you did," Sinclair said.

The medics with the ambulance checked Sinclair's head, dressed a couple cuts, and told her she would probably have a headache for a couple of days, but other than that she was going to be fine.

"I'd like to shoot that son of a bitch," Sinclair said, rubbing the back of her head lightly.

"What was he screaming at you?" McCain asked. "He sounded really pissed."

"I think he thought I was his mother," she answered. "Sounds like he had a terrible childhood and was blaming his mother for everything. My guess is the women he killed resembled her. And I guess I do too. He said he loved her but he had to punish her."

"Great," said Williams. "Definitely a psycho. We better find him."

The medics were getting their stuff together and were about to leave, but they told Sinclair she should take it easy and watch for signs of a possible concussion.

"You have someone at home who can keep an eye on you?" the medic asked.

"No, I live by myself," she said. "But I really don't want to go back to my house tonight."

"You can crash with me and Jack if you want," McCain said. "Jack can be a rude host though. Sometimes he'll crawl right into bed with you."

"I'd like nothing more," Sinclair said, and gave the yellow dog a hug.

It was decided they would leave Sinclair's car at the double wide. It was evidence in a crime, and the crime scene crew would need to come in and dust it for prints, even though they had two eyewitnesses who could identify Stratford as the man who abducted Sinclair.

Once the law enforcement officers had everything they needed from McCain and Sinclair, the two of them, along with Jack, walked slowly down the gravel road, through the orchard to where McCain's truck was parked. As they walked, she asked McCain how he had figured it out. Again, he said he really didn't know if Stratford was the guy. He told her about checking Burke, Stratford, and Teddy Johnson with the sheriff in Colorado to see if any of the men had lived in or near the place when the women there went missing.

"The sheriff in Colorado ran the driver's licenses for the three men's names," McCain explained. "Burke was the only one living in Colorado, in a ski resort town less than an hour from where the women went missing."

"So, Stratford didn't live in Colorado during that time?" she asked.

"No," McCain said. "But when I looked at the map of Colorado, I noticed the county where the women went missing was on the state line with Wyoming. I asked the sheriff to check Stratford's name there, and sure enough, he had worked as a deputy for the sheriff's office in Sweetwater County, Wyoming."

"Hmmm," Sinclair said. "What about the third man? Who is Teddy Johnson?"

"I thought it was a real longshot that he was the guy, but when I was checking on some bear poachers right after Jack and I found the Jimenez woman, he had a single wheel game cart in the back of his truck and there was fresh blood in the bed of the pickup."

"You could have gotten a blood sample and had it checked against the woman," she said.

"Not without a warrant," McCain said. "And Johnson was about to shoot me as it was. We arrested him a couple days later for a list of things as long as your arm. He's currently a guest of the county down at the jail, so I figured he wasn't going to be kidnapping and killing any women tonight."

"And he never lived in Colorado," Sinclair said.

"Not that I could find," McCain said. "The other thing I noticed about Stratford is how he acted around the dead bodies. He was at two of the recovery sites, and he acted like he could care less. He didn't look at the remains, said he was squeamish, and when you showed up at the body of the Alverez woman, he made some smart remark about what you were going to find there. Like he already knew you'd find nothing."

McCain also told her about running into the deputy at the mini-mart in Naches, after he'd stayed on the ridge and watched a rig go up to where he had found the Jimenez woman.

"And that whole deal with him getting lost when you were with him coming up to the site," McCain said. "I believe that was all on purpose."

"Well, we know who he is now," she said as she climbed into the passenger seat of McCain's truck. "We just have to find him."

They drove to Sinclair's house, so she could get a few items for an overnight stay with McCain. He went with her into the house and waited for her on the couch.

"Thanks for doing this," she said when she returned with a small duffle. "I'd probably be fine here, but it will be good to have a little company."

As they were leaving, just for the heck of it, McCain took a swing around a couple of the blocks near Sinclair's house. There, parked on one of the side streets, was Stratford's county sheriff's SUV.

"I'll call it in," said Sinclair. "If that is the vehicle he used to haul any of the other women, there might be some DNA evidence in there."

"You know," McCain said. "If he used his sheriff's rig to pull over the women in their cars, they'd have trusted him and followed orders if he asked them to get out. And anyone passing by would pay no attention to just another motorist getting stopped by the cops."

Stratford was glad he had planned for a possible escape. How the hell had McCain figured out it was him? He knew he hadn't been followed. Somehow, McCain knew. But how?

He'd purchased the Triumph Tiger 800 just for this purpose. The bike was a great off-road motorcycle but had the power to go as fast as needed on the highway. He had ridden the trail many times during daylight, and now he knew exactly where he was going, even by the small headlight.

The trail led to an irrigation canal, which had a dirt service road along it. When he hit the service road he took it to a paved road that fed into another paved road that ran along the Yakima River until it hit I-82 heading north and west.

He knew every police agency in the state would be looking for him, so his plan was to head for the mountains, ditch the bike and hike the Pacific Crest Trail south into Oregon. He'd hike it all the way to Mexico if he had to.

He rode for a couple miles on the freeway and jumped off on the second exit to Selah. That would get him on the road up into the Wenas, then into the Norse Peak Wilderness where he would eventually cut the top of the Cascades and the Pacific Crest Trail.

As he rode, he felt the cool evening air blowing against him and he felt free. He wondered how long that feeling would last.

CHAPTER 26

McCain had given Sinclair the option of sleeping in his room or in a guest room with a bed that was only slightly better than sleeping on the floor according to a couple of guests. She had opted for the guest room, and after sitting and talking with McCain until almost two o'clock in the morning, she went in and immediately fell asleep.

"How was it?" McCain asked when she wandered out into the kitchen a few hours later.

"Actually, it wasn't bad," Sinclair said. "I was so emotionally exhausted I could have slept out in your driveway."

He poured her a cup of coffee, and she checked her phone. Evidently the whole world wanted to speak to her because she had thirty-one missed calls.

"Good thing you put it on silent," McCain said. "So what's the plan?"

"Well, I see about half of these calls are from my boss," she said. "Maybe they caught Stratford and we can put this whole thing to bed. I'll call him now and see what's going on."

After a lengthy conversation with her boss, Sinclair hung up and turned to McCain. She told him they didn't have Stratford but thought they knew where he was heading. The FBI had received reports from people in Selah and out in the Wenas of a motorcycle rider racing through that country a short time after Stratford fled. Sinclair said the sheriff's deputies had checked with all the motorcycle shops in the area and found out Stratford purchased a hot Triumph bike, built for both highway and off-road riding. They had the license number of the bike and were looking for it, and him.

"The only reason he would ride that way is if he was headed into the Cascades," McCain said. "He seems to feel like he knows that country."

"According to my boss, every available sheriff's deputy in two counties is up that way searching for him," she said.

"What about you?" he asked. "What are you going to do?"

"Well, if I can get you to give me a lift home, I'm going to stand in a shower until the hot water runs out. Then I need to answer some of these other calls," she said. "The office is bringing me a new car."

"I hope it's not as big and ugly as the last one," McCain teased.

He drove Sinclair home and asked her if she needed anything else. She told him that she was good and then she said, "Let's get together later."

"That sounds good," McCain said. "Call me when you can."

McCain headed for home, as he had a few phone calls to take care of himself. Word had gotten around that he had figured out Stratford was the serial killer, and everyone from the Director of the Fish and Wildlife Department on down wanted to hear about it.

He was supposed to be on the clock, but McCain had called his boss and told him he'd be late. They had chatted about how the whole thing had unfolded the night before, and his boss decided he should just take the day off.

That is exactly what he was planning on doing, until he took a call from Deputy Williams.

"They found the motorcycle," Williams said before McCain even had a chance to say hello. "It's up at the end of Forest Service Road 1902 near Cougar Valley. He's taken off on foot from there."

"That's some real wilderness up there," McCain said.

"You know that country better than most of us," Williams said. "Any chance you and Jack would want to come up and help us search for him?"

McCain told him he'd have to check with his bosses, but if they approved, he would be on his way.

"Better come armed," Williams said. "We're assuming he is."

"Roger that," McCain said and hung up so he could call his boss.

Twenty minutes later, outfitted in his hunting clothes and boots, with his emergency to-go pack on his back and his personal .257 Weatherby rifle slung over his shoulder, he whistled for Jack to come load up.

"Where you headed, Luke?" Austin Meyers yelled from across the street. "You going hunting?"

"Sort of," McCain said. "I'm going to try to help catch that Cascade Killer guy."

"Cool!" Austin said. "And Jack's going too?"

"Yep, Jack's going too," McCain said.

He told Austin goodbye, jumped into his Tundra, and they headed toward the mountains.

When McCain pulled up to the end of Forest Service Road 1902 there were two sheriff's SUVs parked there. The men were looking at the motorcycle.

McCain jumped out of the truck, followed closely by Jack. They walked over to the deputies, and Williams said, "Hey, Luke, thanks for coming. I know you've already had a busy twelve hours or so, but we can really use the help."

"No problem," McCain said. "Have you found any fresh tracks?"

"We think so," Williams said. "We found some about the size of my boots. I remembered when you tracked me and Stratford to that body and made a comment on our boot sizes."

Williams walked him over to where the tracks were, and McCain took a good look at them.

"Yep, these are pretty fresh," McCain said. "And they're the right size. Were there any other private rigs up here when you guys found the motorcycle?"

"I got up here first and spotted the bike," Paul Garcia said. "No other rigs were here."

"Were there any articles of clothing around the motorcycle?" McCain asked.

"Just his helmet," Garcia said and pointed to the helmet sitting just off the road.

McCain went, grabbed his pack, loaded his emergency sleeping bag and tent and a couple more bottles of water, and set it on the ground. He then got his rifle out, put a cartridge in the breech, loaded four more in the magazine, and threw another ten rounds in the front pocket of his pack.

Williams didn't want McCain to go by himself, so he told Garcia to gear up.

McCain wasn't crazy about the idea of having someone else along, especially Garcia who was, at best, a little out of shape. He really didn't need someone slowing him down.

Garcia had a small pack himself, and he had a YSO-issued .223 rifle slung over his shoulder.

"You got a day's worth of supplies in that pack?" McCain asked Garcia.

"I'll be fine," the short, round deputy said.

"Give us a radio," McCain said to Williams.

"Paul has one. You guys stay in touch."

Williams told McCain that the state patrol was working on getting a helicopter in the air, and they would come and help with the search.

"At some point," Williams said, "the helicopter pilot will make contact with you."

Finally, McCain took Jack over to the helmet and let him get a good sniff. He put his arms into the shoulder straps of the pack, buckled in to the chest and waist belts, shouldered his rifle, put his binoculars over his neck, gave Jack one more good snoot full of the helmet, and then walked the dog to the track.

"Find him, boy," McCain said, and off they went, McCain following Jack, and Garcia following McCain.

Jack had never tracked a man before, and so McCain was a bit skeptical. It was certainly worth a try, however. He figured it would be like tracking the bear that LeRoy Johnson Jr. wounded. McCain could certainly track the man by looking for and following the boot tracks, but if Jack could do it by scent, it would go so much faster.

It was a little after one o'clock in the afternoon. McCain figured Stratford had a big head start. This wasn't going to be an easy task.

McCain had to get Jack back on the track a couple times, but after he'd corrected the dog twice, he seemed to figure out what scent it was that McCain wanted him to follow. It helped, too, that Stratford pretty much stuck to a rough horse trail that led from the end of the road to the Pacific Crest Trail. There were small trails that diverted off the main trail, and McCain would have Jack check each of those out, but usually within seconds the dog would move back to the main trail.

It seemed the only time Stratford left the trail for any distance was to go down to Crow Creek, probably for a drink of water. That told McCain a couple of things. First, Stratford was not equipped to be spending days in the mountains, and secondly, if he was drinking the creek water without some kind of filter, he'd most likely be feeling the effects of giardia before long. Also known as beaver fever, giardia is a parasite that is found in many of the streams in the Cascades, and if a human is infected with the bug, it can cause nausea, fatigue, and serious diarrhea.

As Jack worked the trail, McCain thought about everything that had gotten him to this point. He started thinking about last night and how grateful Sinclair had been. And then he thought about what day it was.

"Crap," he said to Garcia. "Tonight's the new moon."

"Yeah, so what?" Garcia asked, breathing hard from the hard hiking.

"When it gets dark, it's going to get very dark."

McCain started pushing harder. As he did, Garcia fell farther and farther behind.

Finally, Garcia cried uncle. "I can't keep up, McCain. Here's the radio. You go ahead. I'm going to head back."

"Thanks, Paul. Be safe."

"You too. Go get him."

He and Jack pushed even harder, only stopping for a few minutes every hour or so for a little snack and some water. They had stopped following Stratford's tracks to the creek because each time they had, he had come right back up to the trail.

McCain did a radio check each time they stopped, telling Williams roughly their location and that they were still on Stratford's trail. The helicopter finally arrived around five o'clock, and when McCain heard the aircraft overhead he radioed up to the pilot. McCain knew the trail stayed generally in a westerly direction, so he asked the pilot to search that way.

About forty-five minutes later the helicopter was back. The pilot radioed down to tell McCain he was running low on fuel and probably wouldn't be back due to the time of day.

"Besides," the pilot said over the radio. "We can hardly see a thing through the trees, so we're just kind of wasting our time up here."

"Roger that," McCain said, and the helicopter turned and was gone.

Occasionally McCain would take a close look at the tracks in the trail, especially if there was some wet ground or soft dirt. It looked like the tracks were fresher than when they had started. McCain figured that meant they were gaining on Stratford.

About a half hour before dark McCain and Jack came to a ridgetop. The trail followed the ridgeline for about sixty-five yards and then dropped down into a big canyon. McCain figured the trail had to go down through the canyon and come up over the hillside to the west. If Stratford had slowed, which McCain believed he had, and if he was now fighting some of the symptoms of beaver fever, he might still be on the trail going up the steep hill opposite where McCain and Jack now stood.

It was worth spending a few minutes to look across the canyon. It reminded McCain of big game hunting. Search with your eyes. Find what you were hunting, before it spotted you.

He searched hard and finally saw what looked like a trail cutting across the hill at a 45-degree angle. He searched every inch of the trail and was just about a third of the way from the top of the next ridge when he saw something black moving slowly through the trees. At first McCain thought it was a black bear, but a closer look showed it to be none other than Jeremy Stratford, the Cascade Killer.

About the time McCain spotted him, Stratford dipped below the brush, out of sight. McCain couldn't believe he had been seen by Stratford, so he stayed on the binoculars and watched for Stratford to reappear. And he did. The fugitive took a couple steps and disappeared again.

McCain wondered just what he was doing. Then it dawned

on him. Stratford had diarrhea and was having to stop every few steps to drop his pants so we wouldn't soil himself.

McCain was tired of tracking this guy, and he figured at the pace Stratford was moving, even with the emergency stops, he couldn't catch him before dark. He decided to try something different. He got his rifle ready, lay down on his belly, put his pack down as a rest, and found Stratford in his scope. McCain figured the killer was a little less than 500 yards away. Not the easiest shot in the world, but one he had made before.

He put the crosshairs just above Stratford's right hip and then yelled loud and clear, "Freeze, Stratford!"

McCain watched as Stratford stood straight up and looked his way. Then he dropped right back out of sight again.

"How's the beaver fever?" McCain yelled. "It's the shits, isn't it?"

McCain stared carefully at where Stratford had been and didn't see anything.

"You can keep running." McCain yelled. "But I caught up to you pretty quickly. You're not going to feel any better any time soon. Let's end this."

"Go to hell," Stratford yelled.

That's ironic, McCain thought to himself. If anyone was going to hell it was Stratford.

McCain caught a movement just up the trail. When he saw Stratford again, he had a rifle and was pointing it toward McCain and Jack. Stratford had no clue where he was, but he fired his rifle in McCain's direction anyway.

That's all McCain needed. He again put the crosshairs just above Stratford's hip and touched the trigger, sending a 100-grain bullet across the canyon.

A .257 Weatherby has very little recoil, so McCain clearly saw the bullet hit its mark. At impact, Stratford rolled to his left and went down. McCain stayed on his target for a couple minutes, and when he was sure Stratford wasn't going anywhere he picked up his stuff, radioed Williams, told him he had Stratford down, and then he and Jack headed toward the downed man.

When McCain got up the trail on the other side of the canyon it was close to dark, but there was still just enough light to see. The Vortex scope he had mounted on his rifle picked up extra light which helped. He carefully walked up the trail, Jack at his side, watching the downed man dressed all in black through his rifle scope to make sure he didn't move.

McCain didn't want to kill Stratford and had aimed to hit him in the thigh or possibly the knee. When he got to Stratford, McCain could see he had, in fact, hit him in the thigh. He wasn't sure what damage the bullet had done, but it had incapacitated Stratford completely.

To add insult to injury, Stratford had also clearly messed his pants.

McCain checked around, found Stratford's rifle down off the path about ten yards, and let it stay there for the time being. He checked Stratford for any other weapons, and finding none, grabbed the handcuffs out of his pack and cuffed Stratford's hands behind his back.

The wound was a bad one, and McCain did what he could to stop the bleeding and clean it up.

Stratford was conscious, but in a lot of pain, moaning and writhing around.

"How'd you know it was me?"

"Lucky guess."

"I wish you'd just kill me."

"Naw, you can just lay here in pain. You might die, but you might not. You never gave those women the same option."

Williams radioed a couple minutes later and asked for a situation report. McCain told him that he had Stratford in custody, but the killer was in serious need of medical attention.

"We'll do what we can," Williams said. "We have a medivac helicopter from the Yakima Training Center on the way."

McCain got out his GPS, and once it had the satellites acquired to get a good mark, he radioed Williams the coordinates.

"I'm afraid to move him much," McCain said. "I might be able to get him to the top of the ridge. That would be the best place to try to pick us up."

"Roger that," Williams said. "I'll let you know."

McCain had Stratford almost to the top of the ridge when the medivac helicopter arrived. It had been a struggle. He'd basically carried the man up the hill. The chopper found an opening in which to land, and one of the medics came down the trail to help move Stratford the rest of the way to the aircraft.

Once Stratford was loaded, McCain said, "Thanks guys," and turned to walk away.

"You're not coming with us?" the medic asked.

"My dog's afraid of flying," McCain said, and he and Jack started back down the trail.

He radioed Williams again, told him Stratford was on the helicopter, and that he and Jack were going to spend the night in the mountains.

"Roger that," Williams said. "Have a good night."

The view was spectacular from the ridge where McCain set up their bivouac. With basically no moon, and no city lights for fifty miles, he could see just about every star in the galaxy. Some looked close enough to reach out and touch. McCain used a small Pocket Rocket backpacker's stove to heat up a sealed meal of beef stroganoff, which Jack ate in an instant. McCain cooked a second one for himself. They shared a couple bottles of water, and then man and dog climbed into the tiny tent and fell fast asleep.

CHAPTER 27

Stratford was taken to Harborview Medical Center in Seattle via the helicopter where FBI agents were awaiting him. Surgeons operated on the killer twice after he arrived, and the doctors were still not sure they were going to save his leg.

During the days that followed the kidnapping, and the shooting in the Cascades of the serial killer, both Sinclair and McCain had been interviewed by the media about fifteen times. Of course, local reporter Simon Erickson was on McCain's doorstep the day after he and Jack had returned home.

"Dis is da officer who tracked down da suspected serial killer," Simon said. "His name is Luke McCain, and he is also da man who saved da FBI agent from da killer. Can you tell us what happened at da house and up in da mountains?"

McCain obliged with all the interviews playing down the part of the hero. He was just lucky, he told them all.

"Besides," he said. "Jack did all the hard work."

After any shooting involving a police officer in the State of Washington, the officer is put on administrative leave until they are cleared by an investigative team. One day, as he waited to be cleared to go back to work, McCain was driving through Naches and spotted Kingsbury's old pickup at the café. He hadn't talked to Kingsbury or Dugdale in a few weeks, so he thought he'd go in and chat with the old boys.

He walked in and headed to the men who were seated in a booth.

Dugdale was eating a piece of apple pie, and Kingsbury was enjoying a slice of chocolate cake. Kingsbury's shirt of the day was peach with black lettering reading: MARRIAGE IS GRAND, DIVORCE IS 100 GRAND.

"Wow, that sounded like quite the ordeal," Kingsbury said. "You and that dog of yours tracking down the Cascade Killer. And we heard you shot him at a thousand yards."

"No," McCain said. "It wasn't nearly that far. And he was shooting at me, so I just did what anyone would do."

"Yeah, right," Dugdale said. "And that was after rescuing that pretty FBI lady."

McCain decided to change the subject.

"Say, have you guys been doing any fishing lately?" he asked. "I've got a little time off and would like to go catch some trout."

"I heard they are catching some trout up at Lost Lake," Kingsbury said.

"But they are running on the small side," Dugdale said.

After talking for a few minutes more, McCain told the two men goodbye and headed for the door. A couple at a table looked up from their meal and smiled. McCain didn't recognize them.

"Thank you for what you did," the woman said as McCain walked by.

CHAPTER 28

McCain and Sinclair had been spending quite a bit of time together in the three weeks following the capture of the serial killer. It seemed talking about the different aspects of the investigation and the night at Stratford's helped them start to get past that night and the next day.

McCain again told her all about how he had tried to figure out who the killer was, which had led him to Stratford's house on the night before the new moon.

One evening as they were out in the back on the patio at McCain's house, she asked again about tracking down Stratford and the shot he took. Once again, he went through all the details.

"I guess you really are the rifleman, Luke McCain," she said.

"Could we please just let that go?" he asked.

She was going to razz him some more, but the doorbell rang.

"Saved by the bell," she said.

McCain went to the door, and when he opened it an eight-week-old yellow Lab puppy ran through his legs and pounced on Jack. The big yellow dog had been sound asleep on one of the AC vents, and all of a sudden he was a hundred-pound plaything.

"What do we have here?" McCain asked as he saw the smiling face of Austin Meyers standing there.

"That's Bear," Austin said. "He's my new puppy. I named him Bear because I want him to track bears like Jack does. Will you help me train him?"

"You bet I will," McCain said.

Sinclair came in a second later, and in an instant Bear was wiggling and waggling around her feet. She picked the puppy up and was immediately having her face licked all over by a tiny, pink tongue.

"Oh, you're the cutest thing I've ever seen," she said.

McCain turned and looked at Jack, who looked like he would rather be anyplace else in the world, and said, "See how she is, boy? What are we, last week's leftovers?"

Sinclair oohed and ahhed over the little yellow ball of happiness.

McCain went over to his big yellow dog and said, "Just ignore her. That's just how Oregon Ducks are."

Sinclair looked at McCain and then at Jack and said, "I'll get you for that later."

McCain just smiled as he scratched Jack's ears and said softly, "I'm looking forward to it."

Acknowledgments

Thank you to retired Washington State Department of Fish and Wildlife police officer Gene Beireis for his insight and guidance in helping to make sure my law enforcement characters were at least somewhat realistic.

Thanks to Jon Gosch for his patience during what must have been a frustrating editing process. I was only an English minor at Washington State University, so I needed a great deal of help.

And, thanks to all my friends who read along as I composed, giving me the belief that my story was actually good enough to be a book. You know who you are.

A preview of the next Luke McCain novel,
CASCADE VENGEANCE

In this new mystery, McCain and his yellow Lab, Jack, are asked to help locate a lost hunter. What they discover is dead bodies at an illegal marijuana grow deep in the backcountry. Assisted by FBI agent Sara Sinclair, McCain and Jack investigate what looks to be a vigilante killer taking out workers in the illegal drug trade.

§

PROLOGUE

The first sliver of light was just visible in the east when Shane Wallace parked his Ford Explorer in a pull-off high up on Manastash Ridge. He waited for it to get a bit lighter and then shouldered his pack, marked the spot on his GPS, grabbed his rifle, and headed out for the day.

His plan was to walk up to the top of the ridgeline, and then work down it toward a drainage he had circled on the map. There were a few clear-cuts in the area, and with water nearby, he hoped the area would hold a few deer. During the first couple hours he saw a few deer, but besides a small forked-horn buck, which wasn't legal to shoot, all he had seen were does and fawns.

He was sitting up against a tree eating a snack mid-morning when he spotted a bigger buck move through a saddle about four hundred yards away. He quickly found the deer in his binoculars and saw that it was definitely legal. The buck had three points on one side of his antlers, and four points on the other. Shane's heartbeat jumped, and the adrenaline started to flow.

He knew the deer was too far to shoot at with his primitive black-powder rifle, but being new to the sport he wasn't too sure what to do next. He decided to just sit and watch the deer to see where it headed. The buck slowly worked its way through the saddle, feeding on leaves as it moved along. After a few minutes, it disappeared over the hill.

Wallace made his move. He walked as quickly as he could, trying to make as little noise as possible. As he approached the spot in the saddle where he'd last seen the deer he slowed his pace and searched for the buck. When he finally spotted the deer, he was amazed that it was still at least three hundred yards ahead of him. The animal wasn't running and showed no indication it knew Wallace was stalking him. But the buck was covering some ground.

Wallace watched the deer for a couple minutes until it disappeared into a dark green patch of vegetation. As soon as the deer was out of sight, he headed that way. When he got to the edge of the dark green foliage, Wallace stopped and looked at the plants a bit closer. He wasn't a pot smoker, but he knew marijuana when he saw it. What the heck was all this pot doing up here, he wondered to himself. It didn't take him long to figure out the plants were being grown illegally, and based on what he could see, the pot field was a substantial one.

He had just taken his GPS unit out to mark the spot so he could report it when he was hit with a burning hot punch in the chest. A split-second later he heard the crack of a rifle, and he realized he had been shot. He was trying to understand why this was happening as he sunk to the ground, blood pouring from his body.

CHAPTER 1

Autumn in Central Washington was Luke McCain's favorite time of the year. As an avid hunter, it meant there would be some hunts to enjoy in the weeks and months ahead. And as a Washington State Fish and Wildlife police officer, he would be very busy at work. He liked to be busy.

At a little under six-foot five inches tall and a very athletic 224 pounds, McCain was in excellent shape for 38-years-old. He loved being in mountains. A veteran wildlife police officer, McCain worked out of the WDFW Region 3 office in Yakima, which was mainly responsible for the central part of the state. The area he patrolled was huge, with much of it encompassing hundreds of thousands of acres of National Forest Service and state-owned lands.

McCain spent some time in the office filling out reports and going to meetings, but usually he was in the field checking on hunters and anglers. On occasion he and the other wildlife officers, still called wardens by many, would be asked to assist other police agencies in investigations and disturbances.

McCain frequently had his big yellow Lab, Jack, with him when he was working in the field. The dog loved to ride along with McCain, and Jack had, on more than one occasion, assisted in the search and location of injured animals.

The year prior, Jack had helped find the body of a woman who had been partially eaten by a bear. Then he helped track down the woman's killer, who had also murdered several other women before dumping their bodies along the eastern slopes of the Cascades.

It was the last Monday in September, a day off for McCain, so he was planning on taking Jack up into the mountains to hunt for blue grouse. He had worked all weekend, checking on deer hunters in the mountains and anglers fishing for salmon on the Columbia River. He was ready to go do some hiking and hunting.

McCain and Jack were just climbing into his Tundra when his phone rang.

"Yeah, this is McCain," he answered.

"Hi Luke," a woman replied. "This is Deputy Hernandez with the Kittitas County Sheriff's Office. I assisted you last year on a call to run down a poacher who had escaped from the Yakima County Jail."

"Sure, deputy. How are you?"

"I'm fine. Listen, we've been called out on a lost hunter. We've located his vehicle, but we haven't been able to find him. We're hoping you and your dog might lend us some assistance."

"I'm off duty today, but if you can clear it with my boss, I'd be happy to help."

"I'll have the sheriff make the call now. He's pretty persuasive. Any chance you can head our way?"

"I'll grab my gear and start your way now. Text me the coordinates."

The deputy said she would and thanked him.

"No grouse hunting for us today," McCain said to the yellow dog.

Jack turned and followed McCain back into the house.

"We're not going hunting after all," McCain yelled into the kitchen. "There's a lost hunter up in Kittitas County and they want my assistance. Well, not so much my assistance. They want Jack."

"Well, that doesn't surprise me," came the voice of his girlfriend. "He's the star in my book, and he's a whole lot cuter too."

Sara Sinclair and McCain had been dating ever since he

and Jack had saved her from a mass murderer who came to be known as the Cascade Killer. There was an almost immediate attraction between the two before Sinclair was abducted, but after McCain and Jack had rescued her and then caught the killer, a real love had grown. She had moved in with McCain a couple months later.

"What's up?" Sinclair asked. She was tall and slim, with the body of a person who worked out regularly, because that's exactly what she did. Her straight black hair fell to her shoulders, and her dark brown eyes were flecked with the tiniest of orange spots. She was the FBI agent in Yakima and was always more than interested in the daily activities of her fish and wildlife police officer boyfriend.

"Not sure," he said as he grabbed his service utility belt and vest. "They found the hunter's rig but can't seem to locate him. That's all the deputy told me."

"Well, if anyone can find him, Jack can," she said as she rubbed his ears.

Sinclair had been eating a bagel with cream cheese before heading to her office in downtown Yakima, and Jack was sniffing around for any crumbs that may have hit the floor. He paused in his search for a speck of food to allow Sinclair to pet him, and then looked up at her to see if his big brown-eyed puppy dog stare would entice her to give him a bite.

As usual, it did.

"Come on, you chow hound," McCain said to Jack. "It's time for you to go earn your keep."

McCain kissed Sinclair goodbye, and then he and Jack loaded up in his state-issued Ford F-150 pickup, driving toward Ellensburg. He had put the coordinates from Hernandez into the GPS map app on his phone and, while he didn't really need the directions, the app told him the quickest way to reach the hunter's truck.

During the drive up to the ridge, McCain took another call from Hernandez.

"Your boss cleared you to come assist," the deputy said. "We'll meet you at the missing hunter's rig?"

"How'd you find out the guy . . . I'm assuming it is a guy . . . was missing?"

"His name is Shane Wallace. His wife called it in late Saturday night when he didn't come home. He's muzzle-loader hunting for deer, and he is hunting alone. She said he was new to hunting and was very worried he'd gotten lost."

"When did you find the rig?"

"Not until late yesterday. Some hunters noticed it had been sitting there for two days and called it in. The plates matched. We called in our search and rescue team. They searched through the night but have had no luck in locating Mr. Wallace."

"Okay, I'll be there in less than an hour."

McCain clicked off and then, as he had promised, called Sinclair and gave her the details.

"Hopefully Jack and I can find this guy and be home by dinner."

"I hope so too. Good luck and be safe."

McCain had been involved in a few other lost hunter searches. Elk hunters in Yakima County often got lost in the rugged terrain of the Cascades. Most of the hunters were found alive within a day or two, but on a rare occasion a hunter would be found dead. A couple had died of heart attacks or from other medical problems, but one, McCain remembered, had succumbed to the elements.

In general, hunters don't plan on getting lost, so they rarely carry enough supplies to survive a few nights in the wilderness. Especially during elk season when the weather can be very unpredictable and is often well below freezing at night, being prepared with the right items can mean the difference between life and death.

But this was a little different. The late September temperatures had been typical of Central Washington. Daytime highs in the mountains had reached the upper 60s, with nighttime temps dropping to near freezing. And it was dry. Even if Wallace was unprepared to spend a couple nights in the woods, the elements were such that a person should have no problem surviving for a while, even without food.

McCain wondered if Wallace had wounded a deer and had followed it around the mountain and gotten so turned around he didn't know which way to go. That happens sometimes. Or, he could have been injured in a fall. Still, he thought, if Wallace was somewhere in the vicinity, he should be able to hear the search and rescue people who would be whistling and making plenty of noise as they looked for him.

When they got close to the coordinates Deputy Hernandez had given him, McCain could see four rigs parked near a pull-out. There were two Kittitas County sheriff's units, a dark grey Chevy three-quarter ton pickup and a gold Ford Explorer.

McCain recognized Hernandez right away. The deputy was short and stocky, and as McCain remembered from their meeting the year before at a bear poacher's cabin in Cle Elum, she was tough, smart and capable.

He pulled up behind the other rigs, and McCain and Jack jumped out.

"Hey Luke," Hernandez said. "Thanks for coming. This is Deputy Ryan Barnes, and this gentleman is Vern Kennedy. He's the head of the Kittitas Search and Rescue group."

McCain shook hands with the two men and asked Kennedy, "Your people are still out looking, I assume?"

"Yes," Kennedy said. "But we've found no sign at all of Mr. Wallace. Of course, we have no way of knowing which way he went. We've been searching in ever increasing circles around his rig here."

"We got the spare key to Wallace's rig from his wife, and have looked around in it, but there's not much in there that might tell us which way he went," Barnes explained.

"Any clothing items?" McCain asked.

"Yeah, there's a hooded sweatshirt in there."

"Okay, I'll grab that and let Jack give it a good smell. I'll get my gear, and we'll see what we can do."

Jack was not a professionally trained tracking dog, but he had an incredible nose, and somehow he knew what or who he needed to follow when McCain asked him to do so. The serial killer was the first person Jack had tracked, but he wasn't the only person he'd located.

Earlier in the summer McCain and Jack had been called in to help find a three-year-old boy who had disappeared from his family's campsite up near Lost Lake. McCain let Jack smell some of the little guys' clothes and after he found a couple tracks leading away from the campsite, he let Jack go.

As it turned out the boy was only about five hundred yards from the camp where Jack found him safe and sound. Evidently the youngster had crawled into the end of a big hollow log, and had fallen asleep. Jack found him in about fifteen minutes, much to the joy of the boy's very frightened parents.

The search for Shane Wallace, McCain knew, was not going to be quite so easy....

Made in United States
Orlando, FL
12 April 2024

45727867R00133